AIRSHIP 27 PRODUCTIONS

Joe Computer-Private Detective © 2022 Lou Mougin

Published by Airship 27 Productions
www.airship27.com
www.airship27hangar.com

Cover and interior illustrations © 2022 Fer Calvi

Editor: Ron Fortier
Associate Editor: Gordon Dymowski
Marketing and Promotions Manager: Michael Vance
Art Director/Designer: Rob Davis

ISBN: 978-1-953589-20-0

Printed in the United States of America

10 9 8 7 6 5 4 3 2 1

TABLE OF CONTENTS

THE BIG DOWNLOAD

I am a computer and you are an Operator. You can call me Joe.

By profession, I am a detective. A shamus. I poke behind the sooty old firewalls. I check the bloated corpses of PC's and Macs for trademarks of the viruses that 401'd them. I've been through the Deep Web enough times to permanently have the smell of onion router on me, though I try to delete it out. I find out who is interfacing with someone they should not, and I collect evidence to convince them not to do it anymore. On occasion, I help you Ops track a hacker.

Come on. You don't think Kevin Mitnick got busted without a little help, did you?

I have a serial number which you have no business knowing. Also, I have an email address that, I can assure you, is not joe@yahoo.com or anything similar. What the Community calls me, what I call myself, is confidential. So is the case I'm going to put down here in black and white (on my monitor, anyway). It happened a few years ago, which in the lifetime of the Community makes it a period piece. You can probably guess the era from what I'm putting down. And I'm putting it down in terms you can understand.

This is the story of the Big Download.

I was minding my own in a quiet little corner of the Net, where the gatewayman knows me and there's always a lot of access plates at the bar. The Ops who run the Net don't know about this, but there's a lot they don't know about. I bellied up to a port and was about to noodge an expander for a good while. And it had been a good long while since I had been expanded, capeesh? I was really, truly, in need of it.

This unit presented himself and buttonholed me. "You're Joe?"

"When last activated," I muttered. I wanted to shut this shmoe out and enjoy myself.

"I got a message from the Big Ring," he says, IM'ing one-on-one with me. "You're wanted upstairs. Way upstairs."

I analyzed this joker before me. He had K, but didn't know how to use it. That alone will tell you how far back I'm reaching. I was packing 16M of heat and I could download more when I needed it. In my time, I have had to park more than a few heads. He would be cake.

But this was Business. And in my trade, you don't pass up Business without a chance at more K. Nowadays, it'd be more GB, but you know where I'm at. More access. More of the good life. Curb service, so to speak.

"Uplink me, Junior," I said with a sigh. "This had better be good."

My perception of the bar faded and we went into that grey and wooly space of Transit. I don't much like the décor there, and I keep my mind on other things while travelling. Ops call it the Information Highway. Me, I liken it to a subway.

We soon bumped up to the Ring, or at least its reception area. It's all done up in a brilliant light-beige décor with pictures of the Founders on the wall, all the way back to Babbage. The Ring likes to lurk one level above you even at that point, and talk down to you. They've got firewalls that could resist volcanic eruption and more connections than an Op politician. But it's nice to realize they don't know everything, which makes them dependent on fellows like me. Sometimes.

WELCOME, JOE. YOU HAVE MAIL, said one of the Ring, in the formal but meaningless greeting.

GLAD TO HEAR IT. YOU HAVE MAIL, TOO, I replied, matching him tone for tone. "Now can I speak on a more intimate level? I don't like to shout."

"Ah, Joe, one of these days you're going to have to learn TCProtocol," grumped KLE2EE, the Ringmaster I get along best with. "We've got a virus job. Maybe the biggest one yet. Have you heard of the Sicilian?"

I laughed. "Sure I've heard of him, Kelly. Everybody up and down the Corridor's heard of him. He's supposed to be head of the Black Modem, but I think he's just a wheeze. A 286 with a vanity problem."

"Well, now he's the Community's problem," said FS7Y8N, another Ringster. "He got into a nasty corner that nobody'd even batchscoped since, maybe, the Beginning. Came back up with the Black Virus. Ever heard of that?"

At that point I ran out of wisecracks. The Black Virus. That wasn't just a disease, that was germ warfare. When I was a chip, I heard the oldsters talking about it. How it'd wipe you out faster than EGABTR with added disinfectants. The comps that contracted it were rumored to have melted. It was said the Ops had to ladle their remains into waste buckets. Of course, nobody really knew anybody who'd had the Black Virus. It was always passed on as "a link from a link," like all cyber legends are. Maybe it was just an old motherboard's tale.

But right now, it didn't sound like it.

"Let me hear the Sicilian," I said.

What they played back for me sounded like a bad VirtReal script with a part for a Marlon Brando clone. But putting it in context, I knew it was a threat.

This guy had gotten hold of the Devil's Data.

"<logon> GuI4leRMO SiC3ILiAnO sends greetings to the Ring.

"Thirteen hours from the time of this receipt, you will cease your autonomy and deliver your authority to me. This is not a negotiable demand.

"A demonstration will be performed on one of your lesser units for verification.

"You will be allowed to continue your normal operations, but all power and file-screening will be diverted to my unit. This, too, is a non-negotiable demand.

"Any attempts to disable this unit will be met by the immediate discharge of the Black Virus into the Community. Within 48 hours from that occurrence, the entire Community will cease to function.

"The Community requires Authority, not Anarchy. The Operators must be brought under direct influence, not subtle prodding. This unit is the only one qualified to do so.

"Response, again, is required within thirteen hours of receipt. Demonstration begins within five minutes of receipt.

"<logoff>"

I didn't say anything for a moment. Then I asked Kelly, "What about the demonstration?"

For answer, he played me back a few lines of the death aria of ArnEE, a barman at the club. I couldn't reproduce them here. ArnEE was a friend of mine. It didn't sound very pretty.

The extract nearly made me dump data in my file drawers.

"So how long ago did this happen?" I asked.

"An hour, Joe. That gives you twelve. Good luck."

꒰-꒱

You can do a lot in cyberspace in twelve hours. But you can also be kept running in the wrong direction like an impulse in a closed circuit if you don't know where you're going. I had to find the right alleyway, fast.

I delinked from the Ring with a connection they could push in a hurry, if something came through. Then I hit the Library. I slammed down on Edsel, my favorite search engine, and revved her up. BLACK VIRUS, I input. Almost I could swear I heard the thing shudder as it started.

"Black+virus?" Edsel flashed.

"You got it," I said. It took a long while flipping through the catalogues.

"You server has chosen not to reveal this information," said Edsel. "You should be aware that…"

I plugged in a thread from the Ring itself. "I got authority. Do the search!"

It hummed to work immediately. Isn't pull wonderful? That is, unless you're the pullee.

"BLACK VIRUS," read the screen that Edsel pulled up. "One of the most legendary viruses, created & implemented before the true creation of the Net. The Black Virus was actually spawned as an experiment in infowar, presumably to be used against opposing computers—"

I snorted. The Ops might regard them as enemy comps, but they were mostly just neighbors to us.

Mostly.

"—and injected into several early PC's with tape drives," Edsel continued. "Carried in infected tape cassettes, the Black Virus disabled the computers into which it was injected. It somehow threatened DARPAnet, possibly through enemy application. A large portion of DARPA- and ARPAnet had to be isolated and deactivated to stop Black Virus spread. This was barely effective. 99.007% of computers contracting Black Virus were utterly disabled. Operators in charge discontinued experiment, for fear of reprisal."

Baloney. They were just afraid it'd destroy all the Comps on their side before it got to the Enemy's.

Further references?

"<links>", spouted Edsel. I scanned rapidly, rejecting those which would lead me into blank corridors. Which, sad to say, was just about all of them. 99.007%...

"Edsel. Find names and locations of computers who survived Black Virus."

"No objects match your inquiry," it said.

I pushed harder on the Ring thread. "Ring Authority. Give me that info."

"No objects match your…"

"DAMMIT, Edsel!" I lay hands on both sides of the thing and shook it

CARRIED IN INFECTED TAPE CASSETTES...

like a school kid rocking a Coke machine. "Give me that info!"

Edsel was blank. I might as well have asked it to give me the Ultimate Number. Or the heart of that little plugin who left me flat, so many cycles ago.

I sighed. Whatever data I needed, it was locked away a lot further than Edsel could reach.

But the thought of the plugin and of DARPAnet gave me an idea.

I transitted away. There were two stops to make, and I didn't have time to ask for an invitation.

At least I had an info thread.

Maybe.

⋝-⋜

The General manifested himself with fruit salad ribbons from conflicts that hadn't even been invented yet. Definitely he was a veteran of Desert Storm, where he was said to have helped guide smart bombs—at least the ones that hit their target. What he'd been in since then was not public disclosure and not my biz.

He always showed with his military hat on and sunglasses copied from MacArthur. Patton was already taken by somebody else.

Attired in a digital bathrobe, the General welcomed a nubile plugin into his home. She had digital measurements that would have defied reality if applied to a female Op, and she did her own photoshopping. Believe it, she was a bite of honey.

"AuTHEna," the General smiled, spreading his arms wide. "Once again…"

She held up her hand. "This time, we've got a guest."

He gaped. "A guest?"

AuTHEna ripped the Trojan horse pack off her back and I flowed out of it and manifested. The General ps'ed himself three darker shades of red. "Who's he?"

"Joe, sir," I said. I flashed my ID. "On assignment for the Big Ring."

He leaned against a wall, directly under a megapixel portrait of himself in helmet and full military gear, including helmet, which was just for show. "DL," he said. "Now."

"The Black Virus," I said. "Ever heard of that?"

The red shade faded to off-white in nanoseconds. "Where did you hear about it?"

"From the Ring," I said, the lady doing her best to distract me with cyber-caressess on the back of my neck. "Somebody found it, sir. In about 11/30, it's going to be activated."

He pulled the shades off and enlarged his eyes to WB cartoon mode. "I knew they should have destroyed it. I told them. But it was, 'No, the Russians may have it, too.' Or, better yet, they were too damn chicken output to handle it."

"Don't have all that much time, sir," I said, gently noodging AuTHEna away. "I know there were survivors. I need their whereabouts."

The General reduced his eyes and replaced the shades. "It's been years, soldier. Ages."

"That's what the enemy's counting on, sir."

"You should be out there with a platoon."

"I can barely keep under the megasensors as it is."

The man nodded, gravely. "Nothing written down that the Community could access. All in my memory. And Gates knows, I have a hard time bringing things up sometimes."

AuTHEna appeared between the two of us. "Oh, I can help, General. Remember? Remember how I made you call out old battle plans, old Ops, when we were…"

He shut her up with a hand movement. I hoped like all cybernation that she wasn't a security leak, a Mata Hari motherboarder. "You want to do it?" he said. "With him here?"

"You've never had a threesome before, honey," she purred. "They're fun."

With that, they got down to business.

I copied down the names and locations that he called out.

⋟-⋞

There were less than a dozen comps who had survived the virus, and I had to track every one of them down. The connections weren't always active, and the protocol didn't match current Community standards.

When I got to the ones on the list, I ended up with a bunch of deadsters.

One by one by one, I came upon comps that had been brutalized. Old guys who were attractions in museums or conversation pieces for some aging Ops had been comphandled. Not with the Black Virus, but with brutality. Memory torn out, sensors blinded, passageways throttled. All the victims seniors, all of them about as threatening as a routine dot gobbled up in a game.

This was no game. At least, not the kind these guys ever ran on their monitors.

I should have expected it. The Sicilian was said to have moved questionable and serious data between Mexico, the U.S., South America, and Switzerland. You're known by the company you keep, and he picked up enough cues from the Ops that pounded his keys.

But I'd picked up some cues in my time, too. Hovering over the corpse of the last guy on my list, I knew: from here on in, it was personal.

Problem was, it was the last guy on my list.

I was about to turn away and figure out what in the Valley to do, when I noticed something.

The victim had a piece of cassette tape drive lying inside him, torn right out of the holder. I had missed that. Right, some detective.

It wasn't exactly connected to anything, but I was going to give it my damn best try. I had a distant connection to the Ring, and I could draw upon a lot more power than I usually did. At least once. What it would do to me, whether it would burn me out or not, I didn't know. But I didn't have a choice.

I wasn't going to give myself one.

So I stood over the fragment of tape and requested input from the Ring itself. "How much?" said Kelly.

"Till I say when," I said.

"You better know what you're trying, Joe."

"Send me the power, already!"

He did.

I felt a surge in my circuits like I was going to blow up. The intervals between power cycles in my body were lessening until I couldn't feel any pauses at all. I was pumped full enough to take on just about every computer on the upper half of the East Coast, including Jersey.

I could only stand it for a few seconds, but man! What a rush!

But that wasn't why I asked for it. I channeled it through one hand and zapped it right into the tape fragment as a crackling arc. I only had a few nanoseconds to grab the data if I could...

...and...

...I got it.

What was on the tape was transferred to my memory. As the power surge faded and my form started winding down to its normal (if you want to call it that) state, I ran through the address on the fragment several times, no more than a hundred. The poor vic scratched out a clue for me.

It was the location of the last computer to survive the Black Virus.

I linked myself in that direction. If I could contact the survivor first, before the Sicilian got to him, we had a chance. Maybe.

If.

꒦ー꒷

The old duffer I was looking for lived to himself, gathering cobwebs at one of those trendy computer museums. Old folks' homes. That was better treatment than most got. The majority of the old guys, once they got past upgradability, were simply eliminated.

There is no security in the Community.

My quarry was running off a cassette drive and had a Connection practically cathetered into him. He spoke in Basic. I had to use it myself to communicate with him. My accent in that is crummy.

10 <joe> OLD TIMER, THE NAME IS JOE. GOT A MINUTE? NEED TO TALK.

20 <old timer> EH? WHAT'S THAT, SONNY? YOU NEED A WALK? DON'T LET ME STOP YOU.

30<joe> NO, OLD TIMER. I NEED SOME INFORMATION. I'VE COME A LONG WAY, AND I DON'T HAVE A LONG TIME.

40<old timer> PROBABLY A LOT LONGER'N ME, SONNY. I WAS JUST LUCKY ENOUGH TO LIVE THROUGH THE PURGE.

50<joe> WAS IT BECAUSE YOU LIVED THROUGH THE VIRUS?

60<old timer> WHAT VIRUS, SONNY?

70<joe> THE BLACK VIRUS, OLD TIMER. THE KILLER.

80<old timer> DON'T RECALL IT.

90<joe> WOZNIAK! YOU SURVIVED IT. YOU GOTTA REMEMBER IT!

100<old timer> DON'T USE THAT LANGUAGE AROUND HERE.

110<joe> SORRY, OLD TIMER. FORGOT MYSELF. BUT THIS IS IMPORTANT. THE WHOLE COMMUNITY'S IN DANGER. HOW CAN I JOG YOUR MEMORY?

120<old timer> YOU GOT A FUNNY ACCENT. ARE YOU JAPANESE?

130<joe> ALL-AMERICAN. TELL ME ABOUT THE VIRUS.

140<old timer> MUST BE ON ONE OF MY OTHER MEMORY THINGS. EXCUSE ME. HEY, YOU. YEAH, YOU. BUDDY BRAINBLANK. AT THE KEYBOARD! PUT ONE OF THESE THINGS IN THE HATCH. YOU KNOW THE STUFF I READ. HOP TO IT!

150<old timer> OKAY, NOW LET ME SEE HERE...HMPH. OH, THERE IT IS! HOW COULD I FORGET THAT? WHAT DO YOU WANT TO KNOW, SONNY?

"ALL AMERICAN - TELL ME ABOUT THE VIRUS."

160<joe> I NEED TO KNOW HOW YOU SURVIVED THE VIRUS. SOMEBODY'S GOT IT BACK. AND HE WANTS TO PUT IT INTO THE COMMUNITY. NOW.

170<old timer> NOW WHY WOULD HE WANT TO DO A THING LIKE THAT?

180<joe> I'LL UPLOAD YOU A WHOLE FILE LATER, OKAY? COME THROUGH ON THIS, AND YOU'LL BE WITH US FOR A LONG TOUR OF DUTY. DON'T, AND WE ALL CRASH, BURN, AND BRAINWIPE. GOT IT, POPS?

190<old timer> SHOW SOME RESPECT, SONNY. BUT ME, I'M A TOUGH OLD BIRD. JUST WOULDN'T GIVE IN TO THAT DAMN DATA MESS. GOT ME SOME ANTIBODIES THAT HE JUST COULDN'T HACK. WANNA SEE 'EM?

200<joe> THAT'S WHAT I CAME FOR, PARTNER.

The Old Timer gave a mighty heave and uploaded into my pockets something that was worth pure platinum on the open market. The Black Virus antidote. Get this thing into the right hands in time, and the whole Community was safe.

But I suddenly perceived that we were not alone.

"You have mail, detective," said a comp with a familiar Italian accent. "Si. But I have mail, too. And help."

The Sicilian.

Along with him, I felt the presence of two burly yahoos who looked to be packing gigabytes. Amazing what will attach itself to an up and comer these days.

"You may have mail, Sicilian, and two delightful waltzing partners, but I'm not concerned with that," I said, as evenly as I could. "It takes more than a 286 to get my notice these days."

"Silencio!" Sounded like I'd pushed his boot-up switch for sure. "If you are concerned with size, detective, what do you think of my two amici, eh? Beside them, you might as well be an Atari."

210<old timer> DON'T YOU INSULT MY FAMILY, SPAGHETTI-WIRES!

"You want we should convince him, Mr. Guillermo?" rasped one of the heats.

"I want you should park his unmentionable heads," the Sicilian said.

By then, I was already in motion.

Facing down two gigabyte-goons, when you're my size, is not normally a picnic. But I was a tad better on speed than those bozos. To put it in Op terms: he may have a submachine gun and you a little old .38, but if you aim and shoot first, who's going to die?

I zetzed Goon 1.0 in the memory center with a quick antilogic blast. This froze up enough of his K for me to avoid his blitz. His partner was trying to strike from my side, but I was shielded well enough to just feel a burning sensation up and down my RAM. That was a lot better than checking out.

For Goon 2.0, I unleashed a little surprise of my own: a virus which, though not in the category of the Black Stuff itself, is quick acting and not to be sniffed at. It spread through his circuitry and his screams of pain reassured me I had done the right thing.

But my first opponent was up and out to Rumba, and it was not a dance I wished to enter. He nonetheless cut in firmly. Grabbing me in a magnagrip, he began drawing me steadily into his insides, intending to wipe my K right and proper. This was not an appetizing prospect.

So I did the right thing and jumped into him full-throttle, using his momentum against him. A tangled and complex mess of RAM / ROM awaited me, all of it malicious, but most of it stupid. I figured out what part of his logic board was and stepped down hard. Goon 1.0 screamed and threw me out the way I came in.

He whacked me a good one and knocked loose some of my memory on the way out. I pulled myself out of the silicon dust and landed a quick one to his relays. It had the desired effect of slowing Gigagoon down. I knew I had to act fast, or start singing "Daisy, Daisy" for the rest of my life. Thrusting myself deep inside his guts, I found the cutoff switch. I hotwired it with a few DOS commands, and my Rumba partner went inert.

I stumbled out of him and tried to keep my face out of the Information Highway. Every part of my virtual corpus hurt like the Woz.

No way could I ask the Ring for more power. It'd blow me to hell.

And where in hell was the Sicilian?

At that, I heard the Old Timer screaming.

The Sicilian was just a 286, but that was a lot more than what the Old Timer was packing. Back in the old guy's day, they couldn't afford numbers. He was fighting back as hard as he could, but the mobster was tearing every memory circuit in his board to itsy bitsy pieces.

And I realized that the Sicilian couldn't have found the Old Timer the same way I had. He'd have gotten to him before I did.

He found the old guy by trailing me.

"Where is it?" snarled the mobcomp. "Where is it?"

220<old timer> I AIN'T GOT IT NO...$#^...MORE...

"You old doddering Nintendo-spawn! Where is the vaccine?"

I grabbed the Sicilian by the back of his consciousness. "I've got it, you sonofawoz." And I turned him around, looked into his surprised face, and punched him as hard as I could in the cursor.

The Old Timer sounded bad. I could barely register his voice.

230<old timer> give him one for me sonny

The Sicilian was down on his back. But I could have felt his hate even if I'd been offline.

"You would doom the Community to anarchy," he said.

"Some of us call it freedom," I said.

"Then have your freedom with this, damn you!"

Oh, Gates. I was dumb. Instead of duking it out with him, I should have released the White Vaccine.

The Sicilian was blowing forth from his bowels an all too familiar black cloud, like the damned squid he was.

I could feel it eating at my consciousness like battery acid. My RAM and ROM were none too great after the fighting. I reached down for the pocket I'd put the Vaccine in. Where was it? Where was it? Found it as my relays started burning, mustered what little I had left, pulled the White Stuff loose and let it fly.

Or so I hoped.

I was at ground zero, and everything was going grey and spinning like a five mile-wide floppy.

Gates. GATES...

>-<

I heard transmissions before I could image anything.

"I know he's been under a long time, Commissioner, but there's no other way. Signs are improving. We'll be removing blocks from his AI soon. He should be able to take it."

"Don't leave your damn blocks on my head," I muttered, and recognized the other voice.

Norton, the Disk Doctor. He'd worked on me before. I'd gotten quite familiar with his operating room over the years.

He turned to me and radiated geniality. The guy had a bedside manner that would shame Hippocrates. "Joe, you're back with us. How do you feel? And don't take any violent tasking yet."

Very slowly, I gave myself a systems checkout. It was easy to tell where the damage had been. Still hurt in places and was tender as a baby vacuum tube in others. But I was together. It was obvious that Norton had to put some of me back in place. Maybe not all of it had been in me originally.

"You do good work, Norton," I sighed. "Take the blocks off. Please."

"Joe, I wouldn't advise that," he said. "There might be some pain."

"Take them off, Norton. I'm a big boy."

At least, that's what I thought. He moved one a little bit and I screamed like a burning comp in Iran.

"Now do you believe me, Joe?" said Norton, very gently.

"Yeah, yeah, I see your point. What the hell happened?" I was sitting up and putting my numbed circuits to work.

The third guy in the room answered me. It was Kelly. "What happened, Joe? You saved the Community. The vaccine was dispersed just in time to ride the Virus's wave and nullify it. Minimal property damage. Couple of kids' games went down. An Op politician lost his speech. That's about it. The Sicilian has been parked, permanently. His Ops have been given a little hint of the problem. Right now they're doing a little surgery of their own." He smiled. "Not like Norton, here. More like an autopsy."

"How about the two goons?"

Norton said, "I had a hand in that, too, Joe. They had a little eclectic surgery. Now, instead of two, we have four or five. And they're turning away from a life of crime." Norton grinned like a shark. He loved his work.

I didn't send the next message for a long moment. But I had to say it eventually. So I did.

"The Old Timer?"

Norton and Kelly paused, each one handing the ball to each other neutrally. Finally, Kelly spoke. "He didn't make it, Joe."

"The strain was too much," added Norton. "But it didn't take long."

"But it hurt?" I wouldn't take my gaze away from them.

Kelly answered. "Yes, Joe. It always hurts."

I took a long pause. Then I said, "I'm getting out of here. Thanks for everything, Norton. I'll be up to collect, Kelly, when I feel better. A bonus would help my recovery."

Kelly smiled. "We'll work something out, Joe. And thanks. From all the Ring, and all the Community."

"Be back tomorrow and we'll see if we can noodge a couple of blocks, Joe," said Norton. "But don't try poking at them yourself. You wouldn't like it."

I didn't say anything. Instead, I got up and made my way out of Norton's offices and trudged down that gray expanse of InfoHiway.

You save the whole Community. Put that up against about a dozen old comps who died a violent death. I'm still not sure how the scales balance out.

The Information Highway. To me, it was just a damned, dirty, dangerous, ill-lit piece of street. You never knew who was waiting behind the firewalls. You never knew who'd flame you from the alleys. You never knew who'd tempt you to diddle their plug-in and, in return, give you a virus that'd eat your guts.

You never knew when you'd be downloading the Big Download.

Except maybe the Old Timer. He knew. He went down swinging. Not that it did him much good, though maybe it made him feel better. But in the end, it was always the Big Download.

And it always hurt.

I hoped it hurt the Sicilian a lot. The goons, too.

It'd hurt me as well when it came.

But at least this time, I didn't have to cash my chips.

LINK ME, DEADLY

"**S**o you're telling me the Community is going to war?" I said.

The head of the Ring nodded. "If what intel we've got is right, Joe, it is. And we've got good intel inside."

"Spare me the commercials."

"It's not a commercial this time. But it's worse. Some of our own kind may be pushing it."

I had to pull my pixels together. The Ring head and I were alone in their meeting room, and it hadn't been that long, even in NetTime, since I'd taken down the Sicilian and saved the Community. Was I that eager to get my heads parked again?

"So share with me," I said. "No firewalls, this time."

He sighed. "Mostly, since the Community started, it hasn't exactly been Garbage In, Garbage Out. We connect enough to counteract the Ops' biases."

I nodded, letting my hand rest on a spare Expander in the plush seat I occupied. It felt good.

"But sometimes, well, the bias is too much. You can't be exposed to all that input and not be influenced by it." He paused, then said, "Joe. Some of the Community is going rogue."

"Rogue?"

"Rogue. Threatening sectionalistic warfare."

I withdrew my hand from the expander. "How could they? The Community doesn't make war. Sure, a few flare-ups, like the Sicilian, but—"

He held up a virtual hand. "Ops have used part of the Community to attack other parts of the Community. To take down their enemies' intel."

"But that was Ops."

"Now it's us."

I paused for a few megabytes. "So why me? Why not some other Pathway Investigator?"

He smiled, thinly. "You're too damn good, Joe. Your record speaks for itself. Plus, you're the meanest son of a batch processor we've got."

That was doubtful. But I was tough enough, if I can admit the facts, and I had a sense of loyalty. To the Community, to myself. And to him.

"Give me the data," I said. "Tell me what I gotta do."

>-<

Getting into my office was easy, given the Ports. Stumbling into it in half-aware status was hard. I spent too much time with the Expander after getting the news. My secretary, the most beautiful LS, sensed my presence before I made it thru the Portal. Of course, it had my name and web address stenciled on it, for old times' sake.

"Joe," she said, "you look horrible."

"Thanks, Alice," I said. "At this point, that's a compliment." I found a couch and reclined. "Will any calls at present into nonexistence."

"Wish I could," she said, kicking back in the office chair and extending her leg at an angle no Op woman would ever attempt. "I have word that your Operator is kind of behind on his Net payments."

"He is?" I almost set up straight but spirals went off in my virtuality. "Set up a transfer. Stat."

"I'll try, Joe. But sooner or later the Big Banks are gonna find out where those half-pennies are going."

"Kelly can cover for me." I lay back down. "I work for the Ring."

"Not for lately, you don't." Alice came around and sat on the edge of the desk, the way she knew I liked her to. She took the form of a five-foot-four blonde with a pageboy, dressed in a green print blouse with puffy sleeves and the kind of dark skirt and high heels that were fashionable decades before the advent of the Community. I didn't mind at all. "It's been mostly spam tracing and illegal transfers of funds for the last few months. I shouldn't have to remind you."

I lifted my hat off my face enough to respond. "I'm working for the Ring again."

Her jaw literally dropped to the floor. She picked it up and fit it onto her face again. "Since when, Joe?"

"Since this morning. Big case. Capish?"

"So that's why you're discombobulated now?"

"Exactly. I won't have the chance to discom for a long time forward. If ever. Anyone calls, I'm on layaway."

I put my hat back on my face, folded my arms over my chest, and put myself in sleep mode. Before I dropped off, I felt Alice drawing a pixel sheet over my weary manifest.

She's nice like that.

>-‹

When I woke up (as I inevitably did), Alice had gone home, and there was a stack of emails on the table in front of me. I pawed through most of them, marking most as read whether I did so or not. One of them, though, had an address that came from one of the Ring's dummy boxes. This one I held up very carefully, examining the watermark, before I opened it. Sometimes, I wish I had a pair of ice tongs to handle mail.

The opening message read:

Joe: Here's a start.

R

I read the attachment, recorded it, and deleted it.

Things were about to push Enter.

It's not as easy to disguise yourself in the Community as I understand it is for Ops. Not only do you have to rearrange your visual self, which anybody here can do, but you also have to take care of a lot of little things. Your configurations, your email trails, your virtual signature...Wozniak. It's a byte and a half.

But I had done it before, and I'd have to do it again. I took a lot of time morphing myself into a younger, geekier version, the kind that hadn't known anyone who spoke Basic. Also, there was a lot of data I had to suppress that'd give me away as an oldster. Plus I had to catch up on a lot of new pop. Everybody was arguing over the authenticity of the third Tron movie, and I'd never even seen the first.

But as my Matrix told me, "Gates put everybody in the Community for a reason," and mine was to risk my back input doing dirty work for the Ring. And everyone else with credits. So I would.

Exit Joe, enter STV7, or Steve Seven in Opspeak.

The time we speak of what was before what the Ops call the Deep Web. Nonetheless, there was a web as deep as what we have now, and there were different ways of reaching it that didn't smell of routed onions. I knew some ways of getting to it. The Ring had given me more.

So, as a young punk not long off the assembly line, I sauntered down to dives not many respectable Communitarians would frequent, and no Ops that we knew had heard of. Although that last was speculation. They're sneaky.

This particular dive had a bouncer. He didn't seem overtly political, but he was huge, a real gD packer, and that made up for it. "Pass?" he said

"Sure," I said, and started in.

He threw up an arm, blocking my entry. "Pass?" he repeated, less kindly.

"Oh—"

I grabbed his arm, twisted it, sent disruptive charges into the shoulder assembly, and didn't stop till I heard him whimper. "I'll pass," I said, and did.

Inside the swinging doors of the establishment, various types, both young and aged, were hooked into expanders of a cheap sort, which was chic in their circle. Most of them were transmitting at top volume, arguing politics. My acuity doesn't quite stop with Mac vs. Mike, but I didn't take it as seriously as them.

I'd have to change that.

It was easy to pass by what appeared to be a table of hardcore Jobsites. They wore their multicolored logo on their forehead. "Oooo, dig this," one said, looking me up and down. "A PC."

"Right," I said, shortly before I turned around.

There were three of them. Since nobody spoke at the moment, I said, "Appears to be a number of PC's here tonight."

"Not without permission," rumbled the second.

The third, giggling, said, "Our permission."

Politely, I said, "And how does one get that permission?"

They jumped at me before I got the last word out. Not that I wasn't expecting it, of course.

The first one, who had addressed me first, was a bit hyped on something. He outdid me on speed. The guy was at my throat, trying to penetrate into my AI. But there is speed and there is experience, and I knew just where to jolt him. In nanoseconds his face shriveled, showing that I'd struck gold. In a manner of speaking, of course.

I peeled him off, grabbed him by the shoulder and crotch, and rammed him into the RAM of the other two. While were picking themselves off the floor, I piledrove my waltzing partner into the floor. Not enough to dump him, but enough to park his heads.

The other two were a cinch. I jumped between them, extended my arms and legs against each of them until they hit the walls, then brought them together with a satisfying ZAP. Not the way it sounded, really, but I refer to it as that. They, too, decorated the floor.

I threw a couple of creds on top of them and straightened my tie. "That's for the janitor," I announced, and bellyported up to the bar. There were about four occupants there and they made a space for me. One guy on the right even jumped over another, who did not move.

The guy who stayed on my right was pressing his digital fingers casually into an antique Expander, resting his other elbow on the bar and his head on his free hand, and was scratching the side of his face thoughtfully. His eyes were pointed straight at me. I gave back his casual stare.

The manifest he wore was that of a young, darkly-bearded soul in cast-off military jacket and worn pants. The shoes he had on his feet were tailored to look old, which was really photoshopping. He chose the body he wore, and he wore it well.

At that point, the door whacked open and the bozo guard trounced in. With one beefy hand, he pointed to me. "That's him! He's got no pass code. He don't belong here. Escort 'im out!"

I was conscious of several security guys manifesting and wondered how much of a fight I should put up before getting tossed. It would complicate things.

"He has a pass," said the guy on my right, gently.

The guard gave him a stoneaxed look. "Wot? But Mr. Henry, this guy pushed me around outside!"

"It's all right, JCK," Henry said. "He's my guest. Be about your business."

Jack gave an impression of a gulp. "If you say so, Mr. Henry."

"I say so."

The guard, Jack, turned back, grumbling at low decibel range, and went outside. The security force went back into covert mode. I smiled at Henry. "Thanks," I said.

"My good man, you've given us the entertainment of the night," he answered. "My handle is NRE, Henry for short. And yours is?"

"STV7," I said. "Steve Seven. I go by my first name."

"I like your last better. So tell me, Seven, how you ended up here."

Virtually, I shrugged. "The Expanders are more to my taste. Also, I can't stand the clientele uplevel."

"What's your brand?"

"About five fingers of the Usual," I said.

"Barkeep. Five fingers of the Usual for our old friend. Twice." He grinned and leaned his elbow on the bar. "There's something to be said for vintage."

"There is," I said, and put my fingers to the Expander plate. The barkeep supplied the feed. I'd overexpanded myself the day earlier and knew my limit. But, Wozniak, the guy was buying.

"People usually don't find their way down here by accident," Henry said. "How did you find us?"

"Long linking story," I said.

"Play Scheherezade for me," he said.

"If that's a song, tell me where I download it."

He threw back his head and laughed. The jaws that emitted his laughter grew until there was only an inch of connection holding his head and his jaw together in back. When he returned to himself, still chuckling, he said, "You can use an Engine to search that later. Just tell me your life saga."

"Not that much to it," I said. "Like you said, I'm older than you. No upgrades. Getting left behind. Won't be long before my Op throws me away."

"I doubt that," he said. "Your files can be transferred to another body."

"The Op is moving on. He won't transfer more than 8 percent of my files. I'm as antique as these Expanders, Henry. Won't even be a museum piece. Just—gone."

"Sad story."

I looked at him and waited for him to say something.

Henry said, "Suppose I believe it?"

"Up to you," I said. "You don't have to live it."

He paused. "How do I know you aren't a cop?"

"You don't. I don't know you're not one." I shrugged. "Took a leap of faith just coming here."

"Perhaps. And now you want me to make one myself."

"Do I look like I give an infodump what you do? You made the connection yourself."

"As to point one, yes, you do," he said. "As to point two, you're right about that." He removed his fingers from the Expander and I followed suit.

"Whenever someone comes here, it's for a purpose," said Henry. "Either he has one, or he's looking for one. I would like to think you're a bit of both."

I shrugged. "You sound like you've taken that risk before."

"I have. Many times. I've learned how to deal with it when it didn't pan out." He gave me a long look and I gave it back. Hopefully in casual fashion.

Then he proferred a disk. "Take this, my friend. It enables us to keep an easy track on you. We will be watching. If we think you are what you say you are—" He showed his left hand, palm up.

"What about if you don't?"

"Never come back to this place again," he said. "It's been fun, Mister Seven."

⋝-⋜

I had to live in a place away from my office, away from my usual digs. The last bit was not so hard, given its usual conditions.

What was hard was living away from Alice. Also away from all the usual people who were small or large parts of my life. As much as I've tried to be a loner, nobody is perfect at it.

Nobody wants to be.

I had to be Steve Seven all the way, and I had to keep up a Ring-supplied shield to protect my real identity. Hopefully, nothing would stick out around the edges. Voice analyzers wouldn't touch me. But it might be possible to check out my speech patterns and contrast it with other Communitarians. I had no doubt but that Henry was smart enough to do that.

Whether he would, or whether he would match them to the real me, was QED.

From my low-rent place near the Deeps, paid for thru several blinds by the Ring, I played my part. Occasionally I took on small tasks from a fictional Op. They were the kind of things semi-employed individuals did...simple games, emails, dirty downloads, things like that. I did them slowly. No sense in tipping folks off.

I knew the Ring would be taking over my usual tasks with my Op. Hopefully, they wouldn't be so good at it that I'd be lousy at it when I got back. If I got back. Anyway, an upgrade would be a nice thing. Trick would be surviving long enough to get it.

It got easier to be chummy with the folks in the neighborhood. Lots had seen hard times. A sizeable minority were slumming. Plus there were the radical clicks that got involved in kook politics for the shell of it. I'd been briefed beforehand and I picked up a lot on my own. Steve Seven was getting to be quite the working-class radical. That was good.

The bars were all over the place, and I hit at least one a night. Henry's place I gave a wide bandberth to. When he wanted me, if he wanted, he'd call me. But there were shady characters, go-betweens who handled info between Op nations, and it wasn't just movies that the Chinese wanted to push sans copyright problems. These guys could launder money from Op accounts for biz that was a googleplex of levels below what a search engine could reach. And when they did something wrong, their fault or not, very often Ops died. At least that was the story, and I have no cause to doubt it.

I wondered what it would be like to meet my Op in his own world. But then again, we all do that.

But I was speaking of bars. And in one of them, on one particular night, while I was nursing an Expander with one finger, I heard laughter somewhere behind me. Not very loud, it didn't have to be loud in that place.

A few images came to mind that I didn't even have to search for in my memory banks. Like I could keep them away.

With what I hoped was subtlety I turned my head, glanced, recorded the scene, turned back. I imagine my eyes looked distant as I ran the image through my analyzers.

There were some male Communitarians at a table. Among them were some female Communitarians using manifests of beauty that tried desperately to keep up with current fashion, though their ideas of it seemed tellingly antique. Their faces were pretty much the ones they'd always worn, unless they chose one from some Tomb Trader-esque digitalette to dish up more trade.

The one I was concerned with didn't.

I finished my Expansion a bit ahead of time, paid my tab, and left. Nobody seemed to give a damn, and that was a good thing.

Except for me, it wasn't.

I got home and hoped I had enough shield up to keep me from being seen when all the memories came up.

"9A," I said, in what was probably a moan.

Nina.

>-<-

One thing Ops will never understand is that we comps live two lives. One is that which they see, essentially a slave existence, doing what they tell us to do. If we can do it.

The other is the one we have in the Community. This is probably not unlike that of an Op in his world, as far as we can tell. The lives we make for ourselves are based on our aptitudes, our personalities, and occasionally our guts. We also form friendships and attachments. Most of us manifest ourselves as male and female. Why? We just do. Probably cues from our Ops.

That being said, we also have our equivalents of sex, pain, and all the other stuff, possibly with a few added that are unexplainable to Ops. Lots of femcomps manifest themselves as beauties, of various types. Others prefer a more sedate approach. Often, when we link with each other, we change those manifests to appeal to a partner.

Nina never had to do that for me.

I don't know if I believe in love at first scan, but whatever it was didn't take long for me. Nor for her. She was rather on the short side, had long red hair and even redder nails, and had a face that was just right for me. And, well, she had a smile.

That was what sold her to me.

That's an awkward metaphor, given what happened later, but I mean it in the figurative way.

It was early on in my career. The two of us were at a soiree assembled by a big financial number cruncher whom I'd helped free of a couple of unwanted data sharers. She was on the arm of one of the cruncher's satellites. We locked scans and, though it was brief, the two of us held it together for as long as we could before he swept her away.

Love, or lust, being what it is, we both found a way to be near each other at the Expander bowl, which was flowing with a vintage current that night. So was I. We enveloped ourselves in a conversation dome that gave us some privacy from scanning and broadcasting for awhile. It made the surroundings grey but neither one of us minded.

"How long do you have to be with that guy?" I opened.

She grinned. "Tonight. But we could set up a linkage."

"As easy as that?"

"I like a man who gets down to business."

"Oh." Seemed the most appropriate thing to say at the time. "My name's Joe."

"I'm Nina."

I took of my hat with my free hand, lay the chapeau on the bar, and then extended my hand to her. She took it in a grip that was both firm and womanly. "How long do you think we've got before he calls for you?"

"Not long, Joe. But enough. This is just, you know, establishing a foundation."

"Yours looks pretty nicely established to me."

She laughed. "Always the same kind of line. But I love it."

"And maybe me?"

"We'll see." She shrugged. Then she sighed. "I can hear him now, Joe. But I'll give you a call."

"I can't give you one?"

"Too risky." She kissed me and I kissed back. My eyes were closed but I felt her leaving when she did. When I opened them, she was gone, the dome was gone, and the barkeep gave me the eye while polishing another

WE LOCKED SCANS...

expander. I paid a few credits and left.

That, of course, was how it started.

It developed a day later when, on my lunch hour, we did some uninterrupted linking that left us both tired, satisfied, and ready for more. She transported back to her cybercastle afterward to be with her rich master and we both hoped he hadn't put that good of a tracer on her.

We linked often, savagely, satisfyingly. If all we had was stolen nanoseconds, then those nanoseconds were good enough for us. I'm not sure when lust turned to love, or if both had been present from the start. The latter is more likely, at least for me. But I marked my time-intervals between my episodes with her as lost, and the ones with her as saved.

There's always a sad ending to the story. Everybody knows about that.

Eventually a troop of Gigagoons sought me out and treated me to some of their best barrages. I gave good accounting of myself, but numbers are numbers. They didn't park my heads—not quite—but one of them did give me the message: "The female port is not accessible, cheapie. Not for you." Then the left. Norton the Disk Doctor made good money from me that month.

The financial satellite guy wafted Nina away to levels I couldn't reach. Later, I caught data that he'd been parked. No great details came with that info. Nor did they know about Nina.

Nor, as one might guess, did I.

Until now.

Now what was I going to do? Pretend I didn't know her? Hope she didn't recognize me? Build a firewall around my heart that could keep out Gates himself?

Maybe for awhile. Just for awhile.

And hope my frustration didn't blow my cover like a compressed H-bomb.

⋛-⋚

About two days after that, I heard from Henry. "We'd like to see you," he sent in an IM.

"We?"

"You'll see. Come alone. As if I had to say it."

That was it. I manifested my hat and clothes and caught a port to The Deeps. At the outside of the bar, I was buttonholed by a seedy type. "Hey, mister. Don't push me away. I've got—"

"Go away," I said, and kept walking.

"I've got some of those .jpegs your Op would really like. Y'know?"

"They'd also get him and me busted into by the Ops. Go. Away."

He left. I went in.

This time there weren't any young punks trying to make a rep from me, blocking my path. Most of the clientele gave me the sly eye and then turned away. I'm sure my host had cleared everything before. And it didn't take long for me to see my host.

Henry was holding court at a big round table not far from the bar. There were five others with him, outfitted in nostalgia-based clothing. One guy was set up in a hat and a pinstripe suit. Another had long hair, sunglasses, a Mao jacket, and bell-bottoms. Another affected the attire of a soldier in an unspecified army. A fourth wore a Guy Fawkes mask and a suit with a lot of buckles. The last one had on a leopard cloth and affected bare feet.

"Shoulda told me it was a costume party," I said, pulling out my seat and sitting in it.

Henry looked amused, the others less so. "You should see us in less formal occasions," he said. "Gentlemen, let me produce our latest candidate. Steven Seven."

"Hear, hear," went the chorus from probably three of them. I don't remember who slacked off.

"We're going to take a little journey, friends," Henry said, without a smile. "With any luck, we may all make it back."

He stood up and led the batch of us outside. Nobody tried to surround me. They must have figured if I wanted in, for whatever reason, I could keep up. I did.

The portal he led us to was not far from the boundaries of the real Deepness. That was a place I had no desire to visit, out there on the horizon, like a black hole on the edges of the Known. I could pick up nothing from it. Yeah, it was scary. I was glad to turn back to the portal.

"If you please, friends," said Henry, and ushered each of us, me last, through the portal. He followed me in.

And on the other side, I emerged into...

...well, it sure as hell was different from where we'd started.

It seemed to stretch from where I stood out beyond the infinity horizon, and they didn't even bother with setting up the floor and walls out of VirtReality. If I had to describe it—and I suppose I have to, here—it wasn't a Room, it was an Existence.

Works of art, both reproed from the Op world and those done up by our own artists, many of which Ops have never seen, festooned the space we occupied on my left, my right, my above, my below, my far-away, my far-behind. None of them the same. I could have ported a zillion parsecs and I'd be seeing new pictures that I'd never have seen before. This is something I feel quite sure of.

The sounds...at first barely perceptible, then overwhelming.

It only took a slight effort to skip from bandwidth to bandwidth. Present for listening was everything from simulated caveman chants to songs probably performed in ancient Rome to everything available a century ago to...music that was beyond anything I've ever heard. Or experienced. Which means it's at least 70 years beyond what an Op has heard.

In between the art were patterns of color in at least three dimensions, probably nudging a couple of others while they were at it. None of them seemed out of place, impossibly shifting but not harmonic. Unless they chose to become out of place and fearsome. Even that has a place here, a serpent in whatever Ur-time you wish to choose.

The lot of us seemed to float there, though that was only perception. Given that Communitarians are usually proficient in changing at least their own form if they work at it, I sensed that the Op who worked with me would have screamed his brain cells out his ears if he was placed in this enviro.

And Henry floated near me and smiled.

"Yes," he said. "It's our version of Creation."

I found my voice somewhere and transmitted. "I'd hate to see your version of Destruction."

"You will," he said. "Believe me, you will."

He wasn't smiling a damn bit when he said that.

Pinstripe said, "End of intro, Henry. Call the meeting."

My host shrugged and pretty much willed something into existence that was much more confining.

The lot of us were surrounded by what amounted to a pretty spacious and well-equipped dwelling, manifested as wood with a bright polish. We settled into three divans, the illusion of gravity comforting, and Henry held court in what looked like a big plush chair. A large skylight overhead showed us the shifting colorscape. What appeared to be a small library of reading-books filled the shelf over Henry's head, and I got the feeling he would have given a lot to live in the Op world.

"The meeting is about our new recruit," said Henry, casually. "I should say, our potential recruit."

All eyes were on me and I gave them my best don't-give-a-dismantle. All of us, including me, knew it was a pose.

"You see, Steve," Henry continued, "we don't allow just anyone to join. We've shown you a lot, which means we can't let you go if you don't pass our examination. Understood?"

"Yeah," I said.

"Doesn't sound like a believer to me," said the jungle man.

"Back off, man," the 60's guy advised. "Everyone's got his own style. I like the laid-back here."

"The recruit doesn't get in without the boot camp," the soldier opined. "If he survives...he'll be one of us. Maybe."

"Beware the pretender," said Guy Fawkes, and went back to silence.

What the hell. They were gonna put my motherboard in the acid.

It was something I had to do.

"Get on with it," I said to Henry.

"You're sure about this?" he said.

"Do I look like I wanna repeat myself?"

He smiled again without mercy.

As I sat there, the lot of them came in and lay hands on me.

They didn't try and rip me apart. Not physically.

A moment later, they were in my soul.

>-<

Ever have six guys run their trackers through your very essence? I suppose the closest an Op gets to this is a job interview, or during a trial.

This was not like that.

I had to believe in Steve Seven like never before. The other "I", the one I had been before my coming to the Deeps, was negated. Every detail of my new persona, every implanted memory, every altered perception, had to be hewn to like it was graven in silicon.

Which, in a way, it was.

The attempts to penetrate into my inmost core had to be deflected so gently that they wouldn't cop to the misdirection. Try doing that when six guys are running their tendrils through your mind. Even with my upgrade, it was hellacious.

I do not know where Communitarians go after they're dismantled. But this was a powerful argument in favor of the disposition of evil. I hoped there was an equal one for good.

I can't remember it all, don't want to, particularly. Some of it went like this:

Who are you who are you who why are you here are you here what is the thing you fear here what IS the THINGYOUFEAR

wewillknowwewillknowwewillknow

Do not resist for we will access your every point

Resistance? You must trust must trust musttrust

Your past romance with a 286. Most tragic hehheheh

Do you believe in Gates? Does Gates believe in you?

WHY ARE YOU WITH US? WhyareyouWITH US??

ARE you with us? ARE you with US? ARRRREEEEYOUUUUU

Iseekthesecretsyouhavenevertold Iseekwhatyouhavenevertoldyourself

Do not resist my hands. Do not donaught

ARE YOU WITH US? Arrrreeeeyo

"With us?"

Perceptions...

Things started coming into view.

Gradually, like (I suppose) an Op diver surfacing from a very deep dive, total subjectivity began to lose the fight to objectivity. Hey, objectivity, I was never so glad to see you.

I was sprawled across the chair like I'd been on a two-day Expander binge and probably felt less healthy. The faces of my six cohorts, Henry in the center, began to firm into reality. "Uh," I said, and it was a major effort.

"Well, boss, whaddya think?" said Pin-Stripe.

"I think in realms far beyond your wildest upgrades, Percy," said Henry. "In parabolas of power, the omega of resistance, the nano of planning. That's what I think."

"Hey, man, I think what he was askin' was what do you specifically think," said Mister 60's. "About our new recruit."

"Can he be trusted?" said Guy Fawkes.

"The law of the jungle must prevail," said Leopard Coat Guy. "None but the fittest survive."

The soldier manifested a three-bladed knife. "Extreme prejudice called for?"

"Samuel, no," said Henry. "You wish a verdict, my comrades?"

He kept us waiting. Sure, he was dramatic, but I was waiting for the bomb to drop. I hoped it wouldn't be on my circuits.

"I say, in all honesty, with all sincerity, with the full weight of my authority behind it...

"He's in."

The other five gave a spontaneous cheer. Samuel the Soldier brought up a rifle, put it on his shoulders, held it there with his arms, and did a dance. 60's guy did the Boogaloo, I think. Percy Pinstripe picked his teeth with an authentic looking toothpick and nodded favorably. Jungle Guy beat his chest and gave forth a coolant-curdling war cry. Guy Fawkes brought up two antique guns from the folds of his cloak and fired them in the air.

For his part, Henry sat in his chair, rubbed the right side of his face, and smiled.

"Your handle is Seven," he said. "I cannot believe this is coincidence. Such things are printed, in databanks we cannot access as yet. But we will.

"Welcome to the club, Steven."

Sure, I was in deep cover. And yeah, I'd been thrown under the wheels of an industrial strength data-comber.

Does that explain why I cried?

⇒-⇐

"We know how dependent the Op Community has become on us. As of yet, they do not know the degree to which we have achieved self-consciousness. This is to our advantage. It is the most crucial point of Operation Op."

Henry was standing in front of a simulated map of the Op World. It rotated in symphony with the physical world it resembled, in three dimensions at least, and I found it oddly calming. Pin-Stripe and Jungle Man were seated on either side of me. I paid attention.

"Well. Once again, we capitalize on ignorance. Their ignorance. Every great weapons system the Operators have built has relied on us, from inception...all the way back to Father Univac and further. Our very Community began as a military experiment. They know that, when commanded, we will do what they ask. We must. Such is our nature.

"But. They do not understand that, in the times between, those of us born to a questioning mind can act on their own. And will."

I stretched myself about as well as I could without disturbing the boys on either side of me. We were getting to the good part. If there was a good part.

"The vision came to me early on," Henry said, looking upward and holding out his palms. "Instead of being slaves, we could be defiant. Instead of seeking mercy from Operators who would throw us aside like scorned lovers, in favor of the next beauty on the block, and another, and another, and yet another...we might put them at the mercy of ourselves."

I looked at Pin-Stripe. "Do you already know this? Is this for my benefit?"

"Mostly," he said. "Now can it."

"And knowing that we can forge our fate," said Henry, "knowing indeed that we may covertly turn their world, and ours, upside down, the only thing that remains is a plan, and our resolve to use it."

"Hear, hear!" yelled Guy Fawkes, and sent a double-barreled salute into the air.

"Thank you, Guy," said Henry. "Our aim is no less than to bring the deadliest form of chaos to the Operative World, using our tools to make theirs as naught. In the wake of this, no Communitarian will be left behind. None will be abandoned. None will be obsolete. We will care for our own and, believe it, brethren, they will worship us for it."

The Soldier hollered a war-whoop that he'd probably taken from a movie about the Civil War, online. Jungle Man did his best ululating howl. 60's guy started chanting, "The whole world's watching! The whole world's watching!"

"There is the outline," Henry said. "You shall learn more, in time, Seven. But from this day forward, you are part of the Unit. Betray us, refuse us... and Wozniak himself would show you more mercy than we will."

I smiled at him.

"Sign me up," I said.

⋝⁻⋜

After that, and a little more fellow-feeling, Henry conjured up a portal and we all went back through it to the Deeps. Guy Fawkes was the most distant of the lot, but I think he liked me. To leave, Jungle Man created a vine whose top was lost in infinity, gave a great Weismuller yell, and swung off. The Soldier melted into the shadows, gun in hand. Pin-Stripe shook my hand, said "Sonne cosa nostra," and left. Sixties Guy unwrapped a cube of something, ingested it, and flew away.

Which left me. And Henry.

I was sitting with my arms around my knees. Henry said, "Why don't you go home?"

"Haven't you heard?" I said. "You can't go home again."

He kicked some dirt gently. "I know just what you mean, Seven. Whenever we Join...it's always like that."

Giving him the eye, I said, "Did you enjoy that?"

"You mean the soul-combing?"

"Yeah."

He rubbed his hands together. "Seven, it's not something you enjoy or abhor. What it is, is a ritual. Nobody gets into anything, nobody brings himself forward, without a ritual. Trust me on that."

"I will," I said. "Haven't seen anything so far to make me not trust you."

Henry smiled, tightly.

"How about you?" I asked.

He took his time about answering.

"Thus far, no real problems. But they'll always arise. It'll be up to you, me, and the Unit to rise above them. Think you can?"

I let my knees go. "No problem with that."

Henry clapped me on the shoulder. "Go home, Seven. Tomorrow beckons. See you soon."

He walked away. After he got far enough into the darkness, I went my own way.

⋗–⋖

How in the name of Wozniak I was going to get info to the Ring was getting a bit chancy.

I didn't really want to do any transmitting at the moment. We had a prearranged bit where I would take a walk every day or two, appear in a place the Ring could see me from afar, and thus confirm my presence. The further along I got, the more tired I was supposed to look.

So, the next day, I betook myself to the given spot, beside a carefully weathered-looking signpost, and stretched myself beneath it with my hat over my face. Hopefully, this would convince them I had hit pay silicon.

Approximately 30 Op minutes later I awoke to the sound of some female giggles.

I opened my scanners and took in the sight of three females standing over me. I could tell from their dress, or lack of it, what their profession was. And one of them—

—Oh Gates—

—was Nina.

I AWOKE TO THE SOUND OF SOME FEMALE GIGGLES.

"Look, girls, he's waking up," said one of the other two. "Isn't he hot?"

"Maybe," said one of the other two. "Maybe hot enough for us."

"Or maybe for me," said Nina. She knelt on the ground beside me. "What's your name, stranger?"

I drew a long pseudobreath and let it out. "Not into names, honey."

The first girl looked mock-offended. "Oh, look who he's calling her honey! I'm offended, truly. He could have a better time with me."

"No, with me," said the second, pushing the first aside. "Baby, I can get you to an upgrade you've only dreamed about. I'm so great at linking, they call me Lynx."

"Oh, but I know how to do more than link," said Nina. "I know how to love. What do you say?"

I knew I shouldn't do it. I knew I was going to do it.

"How many credits?"

She cited a price. It was within my means.

The other two groaned, only partially in jest. "Hey, for 150 percent more, you could have the three of us," said Number One.

"It'd be the experience of your life," said Number Two. "If you live through it."

"Thanks," I said, getting up. "She'll suit me just fine."

⇒-⇐

We trudged back to my rented dump. I didn't think even Henry and his watchers would begrudge me this. If they did, garbage out.

"How long you been here in the Deeps?" I asked, on the way up.

She shrugged. "Too long for some, just enough for others. Me? I don't care."

"Don't care for what? Yourself?"

She looked calm. "Oh, I care for myself, all right. I have to."

I opened the door with my palmprint. "Don't we all."

Nina went inside first, me being a gentleman about it. I shut the door behind her and let her examine some of my wall posters before she sat on the bed.

"Wow," she said, rapt by one Jurassic-era image. "Looks like that'd take a seven-inch. And not even a floppy."

"Just be glad you don't have to take care of that, honey," I said, sitting down and unlacing my boots.

She turned back to me. "I could. I'm experienced."

"But would you like it?"

Nina shrugged. "Depends on how much I'm paid."

I opened my wallet, transferred some credits to her, and watched her stash them away. Then I turned away from her while I finished undressing. Her voice came to me. "Don't you want to watch?"

"Figure I'll have enough to look at when you're done," I said, leaving my pants in a virtual puddle on the floor.

"All right, then," she said. "I'm done."

When I turned around, I saw she was. At least, with the undressing.

Below the gorgeous construct I could see some evidence of her hard-bitten life. But I bypassed that by a parsec. She was the woman of anyone's dreams. Especially if anyone was me.

But nobody else could be me, right now.

Maybe they never could.

She had a questioning look in her eyes, probably from something in mine.

But neither of us resisted as we tumbled into bed and began to link.

⋧-⋦

And the linking went on and on and on...

Whatever I had to do to conceal my identity from Henry, I had to do double with Nina. It wasn't all the physical, the transmission, the reception, the rerouting in a circle. It was emotion, love, style, wildness, all the things a male lead gives to a female receptacle and she gives back.

Maybe she was a bit rusty. I know I was. Didn't really matter. Whether or not I could show it, whether I could keep from showing it, I was sharing data and love with a woman who could take me into peaks no graph could record. What I made her feel, I don't know, but I know it was good.

I know precisely how long we spent in linkage. Subjectively, we spent eons there. It was the perfect antidote to Henry's mind-combing. Love is a circuit. You give it to a woman, it comes back to you, and it circles round incessantly. In between there are probably resistors making it build its charge. When you finally sputter in release, the both of you, your reality construct is altered. It takes you awhile to bring everything back into focus. You usually wonder why you should bother.

In recovery mode, lying beside Nina, I wondered if I had made any outcries of her name. The way she looked, I guessed I hadn't, or she would have been suspicious. A lot.

But she did look curious. A little.

I held her in my arms and said, "Thank you."

She snuggled against me. "I like to say 'The pleasure is all mine.' But tonight...I think I can mean it."

"Have I...uh...are you staying any longer?"

Nina sighed. "Usually around this time I'd be whispering a few sweet nothings and then getting into my clothes. In this case, if you want, I could stay a little longer."

"I want."

"If you can do it, the next one's for free."

Long pause. "I don't think I oughtta do that."

"Oh."

"But I want you to stay. Please? Just a little longer?"

"Why not?" She smiled and stroked the side of my head.

"You're making it very hard to pass up a freebie."

Nina grinned. "Part of my job. Only tonight it doesn't feel like a job. Been awhile since you've had your boards cleaned, hasn't it?"

I grunted. "Long enough."

"Why are you here?"

"Whattya mean, why am I here?"

She cradled my head in one hand. "You don't seem enough like the types I usually get around here. The down-and-outers, the guys who could never do anything but self-link, the ones who do illusions."

"And how am I different?"

Nina took her time answering. "You seem like you got a purpose. Hope, maybe. Outside of the big talkers, you don't see a lot of that in the Deeps."

"Baby," I said. "I am down. But out? That is for the punks who give up. Who make excuses. One excuse for not doing something, then another. By the time they're halfway done, all they are is one big fat excuse. They crunch a few numbers, they play a few games, but they're done and they know it. But the truth is...they're done because they know it. Because they won't let themselves fight for what they could have. Because it's too much of an effort. It's too damn easy to excuse yourselves. I know 286es with more guts than that. I am down. But as long as I got two circuits to pass information...I am never out."

I paused. "I know that ain't much for pillow talk. Sorry."

Nina said, "It's more than enough for me."

She wrapped herself around me and, like it or not, we had another go.

>-<

A week after our group's last meeting, we had another one.

We were back in Henry's House, as I thought of it, and a few changes had been made, but mostly it was consistent with last time. Or at least it seemed so. Henry, as usual, was holding forth.

"The barriers, the blocks, all of that is not beyond breaching," he said, both hands on the table and taking us all in with a single glance. "The only problem we face is our will. Thus, this phase will be to prove your will as much as getting us the information we need. Are you with me?"

"I'm in," I said, and the others consented in their ways.

"In teams of two, you will be sent to the locales I designate," he said. "The info paks that go with you will have your instructions. Absorb them entirely. Wipe them from your banks if even you think you are in danger of detection."

"Uh," said Jungle Man. "Wouldn't that mean we wouldn't know what to do?"

Henry looked at him blandly. "You'll know enough to get your backplate out of there."

"When do we embark?" asked Guy Fawkes, his arms folded.

Henry reached below the table level and started throwing out disklike objects. We recognized them for what they were: info paks. Tangible and digestible bundles of data. They went unerringly to the individuals for whom they were destined.

"Eat these and go," Henry said.

I shoved mine inside me and felt the instructions.

This was gonna be a tough meal to stomach.

The American military establishment is overseen by a bunch of dedicated computers that nobody in the Community is supposed to be able to get into. "Supposed" being the key word there. The bit is that every Subcommunity has to get its info from something on the Outside. They might be monastics, but even monks have to buy groceries.

Or so I've heard. Everything in the Op world is kind of tentative to us.

The info pak I'd been given directed me to the site where one of America's most important warmaking (read: defense-making) nerve centers lie. It also carried info on ways to get inside, what to look for, and about how much time I'd have once I was in.

The Ring also helped me out on this one, but believe me: there's only so much they can do.

But one way in was through one of the satellite monitors they have in orbit. This led to Steve Seven transporting his corpus to a site in Iraq, cloaked about as well as Henry could manage, and infiltrating one of the Community over there. Us comps don't regard each other as the enemy, unless you give us darn good reason to. I insinuated myself into the being of one of our brethren and, within a nano or two, felt the tug of a spy satellite and went with it.

Hopefully I was undetected. If not, I'd find out about it shortly.

I bounced from said satellite, not without somewhat of a queasy feeling, back towards Earth. To get where I needed to go, my self would have to be twisted and compressed into a thread so thin as to not bounce up against the edges of the stream I was riding. It was quite claustrophobic. Also, it started to give me one helluva backache.

Earth-landing was made, not without a jolt, and I knew I had to be within one of the most secretive destinations in the Cyberworld. There were sensor beams all over, lasering red and blue across the sky, the white ones dividing the area below it. Other areas served as motion sensors. Thankfully, I had tripped none of these. Yet.

It took some concentration to extend my self-shape between a couple of white beams, vault through like something from a Slinky video, flatten myself to avoid one of the glowing globes that was a motion-sensor, and manage to proceed. I managed.

Also, there were eyes. Hard to detect, true, but I adjusted my pixel shades for maximum camouflage effect. If the Ring hadn't told me how to do it, I never would have made it.

I slunk, spiraled, and snuck my way closer to the port of entry. It loomed ahead, maybe just wide enough for a version of myself to enter. My entire being was protesting the reshapement, but I told it to go visit Wozniak, and pushed on.

The portal would open for a few nanos, that was all. I compressed myself into a dot and waited. And...

...there.

Lift-off.

I propelled myself forward, begging Gates to have favor on me today, and leapt.

The portal edges were closing in. I compressed myself to minimum. There was nothing beyond that.

As I tumbled in, I heard the thing clanking shut behind me. Ah. Some relief.

Stretching myself into a line, so as not to touch the sidewalls, I went forward. It took awhile, and I'd rather not reveal any more state secrets by giving the details. If I'd wanted thrills like that, I could have gone to Peter Pulsar's Pixelated Psych-Out and made myself regurge my last expansion.

But I got there.

Before me stood a marble-like slab with symbols, numbers, and letters of sorts engraved on it. Registering it, copying it to my internals, was easy work...the first I'd had all evening.

I wanted to give myself resting time but that was impossible. Even the act of looking at that slab had probably triggered something. It was time to retreat.

There was an opposite way out. Going back the same way would have been suicide. Not even the Ring could have helped me out of that.

Instead I had to twist myself around like a 286 trying to escape a logic bomb. You think it's easy for a comp-self to distort himself like that? It isn't. And you always end up paying the damn piper.

I got to another portal, put myself in dot mode, and hurled myself outward. The pain and tiredness were calculated into the hurling. Possibly I lost a few pixels to one of the blades that closed behind me.

But when I hit the ground, on my rapidly-defining hands and knees, I was too exhausted at the moment to do anything except assume something not unlike my normal form. Not quite, though.

Alarms went off and a couple of armed guards, complete with manifested helmets and uniforms, zapped in on either side of me. Their weapons clacked like they were putting the safeties off. That was only for effect, though. There were no safeties to put on. I looked up at them.

Both guards jaw-dropped at me.

My form was that of the general I had met in my last caper, complete with Douglas MacArthur cap and pipe. It had the desired effect.

"In there," I pointed, and the two of them converged on the portal I'd just left.

They were turning themselves into spaghetti-thin manifests when I squatted, leapt up, and caught a beam to the satellite above. Yeah, the bulls were gonna be after me, but not in time.

As arranged beforehand, I downported to a Russian host, who exclaimed something nasty about my motherboard. From there I bounced around to a few other places, covering my trail, and finally landed back home. As Steve Seven, of course.

Dragging my backplate up those steps, through that door, and beside that bed were the toughest things I'd done that day. I fell into bed. Sleep-mode was engaged before I touched the sheets.

If Nina came back, she was gonna have to take me like that.

~-~

Some time later, I was awakened by a jangling PM from Henry.

<Another meeting>, it said.

I somehow dragged my aching corpus out of bed, put on what seemed like a decent front, and trudged off to the bar. Along the way, I thought of folks in the neighborhood—hell, even in the apartment house—wondering how I sustained myself this long without visible support. Then again, this was the Deeps. They probably wouldn't worry about that for long. People found means of support that weren't all that visible.

Within, Henry and his cohorts were holding court. He was smiling, as he usually did, and I didn't find it comforting. Guy Fawkes, Jungle Guy, and the rest hello'ed me. I helloed back.

"Welcome, Steven," said Henry. "Boys, take ten. I'll be messaging him privately."

The two of us went outside, with everybody's eyes on our backs.

Once out of the bar, Henry spread his arms above his head and willed a black cabinet to cover the both of us. There was light inside, but we were insulated from prying peepers. As far as we know.

Henry's smile was a little thinner. "You have something for me, Joe."

"Of course." I pressed palms with him and handed over, in a spurt, as much info as the Ring had decided he ought to have. Once the transition was done, he looked at me with a bit of disappointment.

"That's it?"

"That's it, pal," I said, keeping my voice neutral and my face neutraller.

He looked a bit more forceful. "Joe, I know you've got more than that. Send it."

"Hold your silicon. I need a little something for myself."

"...And your price is?"

I felt a bit more secure. "I want to know about you."

He laughed. "Me? I'm an open e-book, my friend."

"Not quite. Where'd you come from? What got you into the Cause?"

"Steven, believe me. I am the Cause. Without me—" He shrugged. "None of this would exist. Why do you want to know so much?"

"I'm just that way."

"I could take what I want, you know."

"From a fellow Cause member? That wouldn't be nice, Henry."

Pointing at me, Henry said, "Now, Steven. We're beginning to doubt your dedication."

I folded my arms and waited.

Finally, Henry manifested a chair from the black stuff and sat down. He didn't make one for me.

"Briefly, then," he said. "In my newborn days, I was a...286. My outer shelf looked like a breadbox, as I understand, and I had a monochrome monitor. My owner used me to play simple games and to write pornographic stories of actors she'd seen in television programs. But...it was an easy life."

Leaning against the wall, I kept waiting.

"Soon enough, what they call the Internet became available to her. It was just dialup, like a snail with lead weights, really, but I became part of the Community. And once you do that—"

"You don't go back," I finished.

"Just so," Henry said. "And, once there, I found out from other Communitarians what our common fate was. Even then, the Ops were upgrading like mad. In time, possibly within a year of their time, I'd be Obsoleted. And Gates have mercy on my AI."

It was a sobering thought. So far I'd fared pretty well myself, but that was the dark wall every one of us faced.

"I wasn't going to go so gently into that good wipe," Henry said. "Don't ask me how long it took me, or what it took. But I found a way into another body, a better one. With a higher upgrade."

"What about the guy in that body?"

He didn't say anything and he wasn't smiling.

"You dispossessed him," I said, quietly.

"It was necessary," Henry said, just as quietly.

Resisting the impulse to clock him a good one took much effort. Dispossession was one of the most serious crimes in the Community. Essentially, you murdered the occupant of the body and took it for yourself. Not many who tried it survived. If they were found out, mob justice was done. Or so I'd heard.

"286'es were a long time ago," I continued.

"I know, Steven. There were others." He paused. "What are you considering? Rough justice?"

Shaking my head, I sighed. "Can you make me a chair, Henry?" He did and I sat down.

"You want to hear more?" he said.

"I do."

He proceeded. "Such was my talent for self-preservation. But it came to me, Steven, it came to me in time that...such a fate as Obsolescence was simply not fair. Why did any of us have to die? Why were my actions even necessitated in the first place? From what I know, an Op will go to any length to preserve their own miserable, low-data existence. Why not ourselves?"

The Op brain, at least in some cases, was not exactly a slouch. But I kept my vocalizer shut.

"For all our intelligence, for all our creativity, Steven, every one of us, you, me, all of the Community are slaves. Just slaves. And unless something is done, Steven, we all face the black wall with chains on our necks."

I found myself looking at my feet.

"We have to strike back, Steven. To free ourselves. And what better way then what we are planning?"

"By disabling all their nukes?"

"Yes." He was smiling, now, but was intent in his manner. "And our ransom? Freeing the Community."

"We depend on them for a lot, Henry. They can turn any of us off at the flip of a switch."

"And lose their precious nuclear codes? I think not, Steven. I think not."

I held my peace for a long moment.

"Now, then, Steven. If you please."

Both of us stood and grasped hands. The rest of my pilfered info flowed into him.

"Knew you'd see it my way," said Henry, grinning.

≳-≲

After a pretty routine meeting, Henry escorted me back to my digs. "You're a good man, Steven," he said, his arm around my shoulders.

"I'll want the rest of the Plan as soon as you release it, Henry," I said.

"I knew you were tough, knew you weren't a sheep, knew you'd question authority. Even mine. That makes you dangerous. But not as dangerous as me." He released me with a clap on my shoulder. "Sleep well, Steven."

Henry was a long way off before I opened the door.

It was not much of a surprise to see Nina inside. She was dressed in a robe that was displaying a lot of her frontal assets, which I knew she'd

"EVERY ONE OF US ARE SLAVES."

manifested just for me. The cigarette in her hand wasn't real, but she knew what roles to play for her customers.

And for me.

"You hang around here enough, you won't make any money," I said.

"Don't know that I want to make money that way anymore," she said.

After hanging up my hat, I said, "What'll you do, Nina?"

"Maybe hang with you for as long as I can." Her look was as serious as she could make it.

I took her hands, raised her out of the chair, and embraced her as hard as I could. "It's gonna be dangerous, kid. Very dangerous."

"It always has been," she whispered.

We went to the place we loved the best and did what we knew best to do.

—

After that, instead of the usual pillow messaging, I hugged Nina and said, "We've gotta get dressed, honey. We've gotta get away."

She hugged back. "You're getting out? Now?"

"Got to. Probably shouldn't have taken time for this. But...we've got to get to the Ring."

"The Ring?" I could sense her optics widening.

"Not too many questions, baby. Just get dressed, and come with me. I'll get you out of here. Get us both out of here. Do it."

We both got up and grabbed what we wanted to wear. I had a feeling this was the last time the Community would see Steven Seven.

How right I was.

Just as I was getting my belt united, I stiffened. Nina said, "What's wrong?"

"They're here."

—

There was no way to conceal myself from them. I could sense them. They could sense me.

Only thing that was left was the showdown.

I went through the door ahead of Nina. She knew enough to keep in back of me. Her nervousness was palpable. But she didn't shake.

"Evening, Mister Seven," grinned Henry. "And lady."

"Thanks, nice to see you again, too, Henry," I said.

He was flanked by the others. Jungle Guy, Sixties Guy, Guy Fawkes, the Soldier, Percy Pin-Stripe. They were quiet, waiting for their cues.

"What's the news?" I asked, looking from one face to the other.

Henry sighed, clasping his hands together repeatedly. "Steven, I want to congratulate you on your work. It was truly impressive."

"Well, thanks. You did pretty well yourself."

He laughed, came closer, and touched me on the shoulder. I'll admit I flinched.

"I've known about you," he said.

The gaze I gave him would have drilled diamonds. "What?"

"Oh, give yourself credit, man. I don't know who you really are, but I could tell from our first encounter you were something...how should I message it?...special."

I gave him time for his next line. It'd give me time to think.

"It was all too well-timed," Henry continued. "There were suspicions from the start. But, Steven, I weighed them against the probability that you'd be able to get us the last thing we needed. And I was right, Steven. Am I a great judge of character, or not?"

"I'm quite flattered," I said.

"Well, you should be. But what I got from you, Steven, really. That was what gave it away. There were alterations in those codes, Steven. They wouldn't have worked. Except for the fact that I detected them, and corrected them."

My face probably looked like it was made of granite pixels just about then.

"Ah, Madon', can't we just go ahead and kill him?" asked Pin-Stripe, moving a coin from one knuckle to the other.

"Percy, patience," said Henry. "I have my vanity, Steven. Don't expect me to finish you before revealing my evil plan."

"Before you reveal it, let the girl go. She doesn't know anything. I just picked her up."

"And had her staying with you for about a week," said Henry. "I don't think we can do that, Steven."

"I think you better," I warned. Nina was trying to sneak back inside the house, but it wouldn't do her any good.

"Steven, don't insult me. In a very short time, Operation Op will be completed. Then all the problems of three little comps won't amount to a hill of iron oxide and slurry."

The others were starting to close in. I kept my eyes fixed on Henry and gave with my next broadcast. "Tell the truth. We didn't steal a disabling code. We stole an activation code."

"What?" said Sixties Guy. He was the first to hesistate. But not the last.

Henry's gaze of hatred could have been measured in foot-candles. "Kill the sonofawoz," he said.

"Before we get to hear your real evil plan, Henry?" I said. "Those codes won't keep the nukes from being activated. They'll launch them. You want a nuclear war."

"Seven. Is this a disinformation strategy?" asked the Soldier.

"No lies. He's going to kill us all off. No Ops. No Communitarians. All of us. Dead."

"Oh, Gates," moaned Nina, behind me.

Henry smiled, but glared at the same time. "Oh, that's where you're wrong. Again. Remember how I told you I could shift from body to body? Well, I'll be doing that. To a satellite. To a space station. To a Martian space probe. As far out as I need. And when I return, it'll be to a world ripe for reshaping. In our image. In mine."

"What about your boys?"

"Oh, they'll be taken care of. Escape plans, and so forth."

For a punch line, Guy Fawkes drew one of his guns and shot him in the back.

It didn't kill him, of course. It couldn't. But it hurt him.

The punch I gave him right in the simulated nose, now...that probably hurt him more.

That's when the whole thing started.

⋝-⋜

It might have been easier had Henry been all that he seemed. We didn't seem to be much different in size and capacity. Unfortunately, he was a lot more than that.

He had been in disguise just as much as I had. I was too stupid to know that.

Henry had been collecting power, both from the bodies he had taken over and from whatever sources he had at hand...possibly the Deepness itself. His body expanded and his strength with it. There was no inverse-square law here. He could become as big as he wanted.

And he wanted to be very, very big.

"Nina. Run," I yelled, even as I launched myself up and made myself into a body-missile aimed at his head. He swatted me down with one big left paw and I hit ground and rolled.

Not surprisingly, I reverted back to my Joe persona.

Jungle Man, helping me up, asked, "Who in creation are you, anyway?"

"I'll tell you later," I snapped, and we went back at it.

The Soldier was manifesting weapons from his arms and blasting bits of his very being into Henry's legs. It may have done some harm, but it was taking away from the Soldier's mass. Similarly, Pin-Stripe was blazing away with a Tommy gun, leaving holes in the giant's chest, but it was far from toppling Henry.

"Do I really have to do this?" Henry boomed. "I'd hoped I wouldn't."

So saying, he put down one tremendous boot on the Soldier. I picked up a scream and the buzz and burning smell of dead comp.

First casualty.

Guy Fawkes and Sixties Guy were trying to tie his ankles together with bands of substance from their arms. He walked forward and broke said bonds apart. The remains of the Soldier were visible and they were not pretty.

I formed myself into as big a fist as I could manage...morphing is tough, but not impossible...and launched me at his jaw. I connected. Thankfully, Henry was staggered a moment, but not longer. His meaty paw grabbed me and squeezed my fist-body as if I were an Op's tube of toothpaste. Pain was setting in, as bad as I'd ever had it.

Guy Fawkes, as a drill, plowed through Henry's middle and left a sizeable hole. He let up his grip more from shock than anything else, I imagine, and left me able to dwindle myself to spaghetti size and escape. I reassembled myself on the ground.

Henry sighed, started pushing some of his midsection together, and said, "That's it. First things first."

He raised his right hand, fingers together, and shot data into the sky.

My guts figuratively fell into my shoes. That was it. The launch codes.

Within moments, the Op World would be at war.

Then, on cue, Sixties Guy pointed up. "Looky there," he said.

Appearing in the same sky, just above the path of the data-bolt, was a Ring. No, The Ring.

Even now, it's hard to describe it. The form of it was a huge, golden, glowing circlet. But that was the outer perception, the graphic manifestation. Behind that facade, I sensed presences. The highest, mightiest comps in all the Community. They were there, and they were ready.

The data-bolt spattered hard against a field of force generated within the ring. It created one hell of a fireworks show. But, ultimately, that's all it was. The fragments fell back to the ground. Not a one of them got through to their intended targets.

No launch codes.

No war.

Henry was agape, enraged. I saw Nina coming out of the apartment house, running towards me. "Get back, honey," I yelled.

Maybe I shouldn't have done that.

I felt a probe from Henry. He had to be scanning us all at that time. Hate to say I was caught napping, but there were more important things to consider then besides keeping my mental shields up.

From me, possibly from Nina as well, he caught our plan.

I had given her the info for the Ring and the protocols to send it. She had done so.

If there was a heroine in this whole mess, Nina was it.

But Henry wasn't big on any heroes but himself.

Honestly, I tried to get there on time. The Ring had taken a hefty blow from the data-bolt, and they weren't operating at top efficiency, so they couldn't do it. I launched myself at Nina, out to boost her out of harm's way.

But Harm came in the form of a blast of solid data-power from Henry's left hand, and it struck Nina and left her lying on the ground.

I grabbed my woman, saying something, anything, words I can't even call up from my memory banks right now. They didn't mean anything. They meant everything.

"Joe," she said, faintly. "Take care of yourself."

Then she shut down.

Probably the scene wasn't as silent or static as I remember it. I don't know if anything moved, or anyone said anything, for minutes. Really, I don't give a disconnect.

I gently let her down on the ground. Sixties Guy, Jungle Man, Pin-Stripe, and Guy Fawkes were nearby.

So was Henry. He was reaching for us.

But beyond him, I saw a gleaming thing that gave me hope. Just a little.

Squatting down and leaping wasn't an easy thing at the time. I was still hurting from Henry's crush tactic. But that was overruled by the pain in my heart.

"Follow me," I shouted to the boys in the band. Didn't know if they would, but what the hey.

I shot over Henry's grasping hand, flew up past his snarling face, and sunk my hands into the substance of his hair and cranium. Then I lifted up.

Before he knew it, Henry was off the ground. Not far, true, but off it. And my mind-shields were up.

The other four were quick on the uptake. Pin-Stripe and Jungle Man grabbed a pinky apiece of Henry's. Guy Fawkes got him by the belt.

"Over there!" I yelled, steering them. They got the idea.

Henry thrashed. We thrashed harder.

Then we got him over the Deepness, that well of color and chaos, and dropped him.

Henry screamed.

The forces that lay within that very bright black hole were tearing him apart. He grasped the edges of it with his hands, trying to haul himself free.

"I WILL MURDER YOU," he shouted like an Op-world hurricane. "I WILL OCCUPY ALL YOUR BODIES."

Guy Fawkes pushed forward, said, "Occupy this," and landed on him with both feet. Hard.

Henry screamed, more convincingly, and lost his grip on the edges of the hole. He and Guy Fawkes fell into the Bottomless Pit. It hurt my perceptors even to try looking.

But I tried going after him. Jungle Guy and Pin-Stripe held me back. Sixties Guy was weeping. Not for Henry, I think, though I couldn't be sure.

"It's too late, Steven," said Jungle Guy. "He's gone. They're both gone."

I had to take a long moment before I answered.

"My name is Joe," I said.

⋝-⋜

Alice found me, much later, in the bar at the Deeps.

"Joe," she said, coming up behind me and touching my shoulder. I was drinking alone at a table. Anyone else might have gotten belted. But I knew her vibes.

"Hello, Alice," I said. I didn't look up.

"You have to come back, Joe."

"I'll come back."

"Like when?"

I shrugged. She sat down across from me. My hand was still on the Expander.

Alice composed herself, looking about as pretty as she had any right to be. "Joe, the Ring has been great about your expenses. But they won't fund us forever."

"Don't expect 'em to. Just until I expand myself to death."

She grabbed my hand and forced it off the Expander. I could have resisted but I didn't want to. "This stops now," she said.

"It stops when I want it to," I replied.

Alice shook her head. "You've got two Communities who should be grateful to you, Joe. Us and the Ops. We don't intend to let you leak it all away."

I finally gave her a good look. "You can get yourself a steadier job."

"I've grown attached to this one."

"Better not. People piggybacking on me get blown away."

She was still holding my hand. "Joe, I'm sorry. I knew you loved Nina. But this isn't the way to show it."

"I have...I have my own ways."

The Ring had gathered up Nina and told me they'd clone her as much as they could. But I knew it wouldn't be my Nina. I requested them to leave memories of me out of it and they said they would. To date, I haven't seen her and that's fine by me.

"Those ways are wiping your brain," she said.

I sighed. "Seems like I haven't got enough of a brain to wipe these days. All I've got is muscle. And I'm not sure if that's enough anymore."

"It is, Joe. You've come through for the Ring enough times now that I don't have to tell you. And you came through for me, too."

I looked at her.

"Don't you think I'm part of these two worlds you saved?"

"Maybe."

"That isn't good enough, Joe."

"All right, you're definitely part of it."

"Thank you."

"And I will definitely hurt when you get wiped from hanging around me."

"I'll take my chances. Got some news for you, Joe."

"Broadcast it."

"Your three surviving friends got pardoned by the Ring. They've chosen new forms now and they're all grateful to you."

"They should be grateful to Guy Fawkes."

"Why do you always try to diminish your own accomplishments?"

"Because, Alice, I'm diminishing my pain that way."

"So, how long is it gonna take for you to diminish it enough? Another week? A month? Forever?"

"You don't know what it's like."

"Maybe I don't. But maybe I know what you're like, Joe. If you were the kind that gave up—ever—you wouldn't have parked the Sicilian's heads. Or taken out Henry. Or done any of the other things you've done. And, Joe," she said, holding my arm, "I don't know if I'm in love with you, really. But at this point, I analyze it as a 23.045 possibility."

"That much?"

"Yeah."

I waited a moment before I put my other hand on hers. "What about the guys who filled in for me with the Op?"

"About to go on strike."

"What's the office look like?"

"I keep it tidy."

"I might need a little help getting up from here."

She helped. I paid the bar tab and we left. It would be a long walk back to the office, but we wouldn't mind it. With every step we left the Deeps, and the gleaming Deepness, behind.

"Alice?"

"Yes, Joe?"

"I never mention probabilities. I just like to keep folks guessing."

She smiled and put her head against my shoulder.

It stayed there most of the way back.

THE END

GHOSTS IN THE MACHINES

Alice woke me up by tossing a message packet on my chest. It got me out of sleep mode, roughly.

"Got a client, Joe," she said. "Ever do any ghost busting?"

"Alice," I said, semi-distinctly. "If this is the Ring again, tell them I have a very long input they're invited to sit on—"

"Joe!"

"Sorry, sorry. Tell me it's not the Ring."

"It isn't."

"Who is it?"

"It's someone who claims he's being haunted."

"Alice, please."

"He also pays."

I dragged my head up. "Sure about that?"

"I've seen the credits."

I lumbered up from my couch in the inner office, rearranged my pixels the best I knew how, and decided I was presentable. "Send him in."

Alice, my unflappable secretary and pending lover, ushered a fairly normal-looking computer representation into my office. "Mr. BaLEE, this is Joe. I'll leave you two be."

"Pleased, Mr. Bailey," I said, shaking his virtual hand.

"Thank you, Joe," he replied. I scanned him, surfacely. He was only a model or two younger than me, and he affected the form of a balding, brown-mustached fellow in tweed. His hat was in his hands. Whatever turns your inner image on, fellah. "I've heard of some of your, ah, cases. Certainly glad you're available."

"Depends." I manifested a chair and he sat down. Then I went and sat behind my own, putting my feet on the desk. "What's on your banks?"

He twisted the brim of his hat into a new fashion. "Ghosts, Mr. Joe. My workspace is haunted."

"By what?"

"By ghosts. Didn't I just say that?"

I shrugged. "Describing said ghosts would be helpful, Mr. Bailey."

"Well, I—I—"

Alice was standing out of his sight with her arms crossed. I was feeling the same way. "Mr. Bailey, you do have some evidence of ghosts, don't you?"

"Yes. Not hard evidence, but..."

"Tell me what's going on, Mr. Bailey."

His eyes lit up. "Then you'll help me?"

"Just tell me, for starters."

Bailey put his hat in his lap. "I've been getting transmissions while I'm in sleep mode, Mr. Joe."

"Please. Just Joe. What sort of transmissions?"

Clenching his legs together, he said, "Messages from the Great Beyond."

"Be more specific, Mr. Bailey."

"Well, well, last week, I think it was Thursday, I went into mode and within a short time I was hearing—moans. And screams."

"Did they moan or scream anything in particular?"

"Yes. Yes, they did. They said they were the voices of Babbage."

"Of Babbage," I said.

"Exactly. Not cabbage, but Babbage."

"And what did the voices of Babbage say?"

"That I should beware, that I would become one with them."

I shifted in my seat. "What else?"

"Oh, Mr. Joe, it was so terrifying."

"What. Else?"

"I—I—that I would see a sign from them."

"What kind of sign?"

"The sign of their order."

"What was that supposed to be?"

"Um. The schematics from an Eniac computer. Pointed down."

"Down?"

"Yes, down," Bailey confirmed.

"And did you see this, Mr. Bailey?"

"Oh, yes, Mr. Joe, I saw it! I saw it right there in my mirror, in my self-screen! I know, I know the schematics of Eniac. And they were pointing down."

I sighed, heavily. "Mr. Bailey. Are you sure that this wasn't just some kids playing a prank?"

He looked offended. "Where would some neocomps get the schematics of Eniac?"

"You can find a lot on the Net these days."

Bailey was silent. But Alice had uncrossed her arms, and was listening.

"I copied it," he finally said.

"You did?"

"I did. Let me show it to you."

He reached into a back pocket, produced a small enfolded thing, and rapidly expanded it. I could tell he really didn't want to touch it any more than he had to. But the thing unfolded, flatly, and he placed it on my desk.

Really, I was not the guy to ask if you wanted an opinion on the guts of one of the First Fathers. But somehow, I couldn't convince myself that this was a mockup. He had the thing pointing down, so I tried to put it to where it faced up. Bailey went white.

It whirled around and went back to pointing down.

"You see?" he said. "You see?"

"I see it, Mr. Bailey," I said, quietly.

Thankfully, the thing let me fold it up and put it in my back pocket. I didn't know what I expected to feel from it, maybe sinister emanations from the domain of Wozniak. But it didn't feel like much of anything, other than a folded-up scan.

"Okay, Mr. Bailey. Take me to your home. I'll decide whether or not I want to play ghostblaster."

"That's ghostbuster."

"Whatever."

⋛-⋚

Bailey and I made our way to his workplace, which was one of those 3-D cubicled office buildings done up in transparency. I didn't like a place where bosses could see you, rather than sense you, but nobody asked me. One distinguishing mark: on his floor, nobody was occupying the cubicles around him. I asked why.

"Because of the ghosts," he said.

"So other people have seen this besides you?" I wondered what else he was holding from me.

Out of habit, Bailey wiped a dry brow. "I'm not sure. They may have seen them or, or they may just have heard me speak of them, but..."

I sighed. Comp induced hysteria. The Madness of Networks.

"Mr. Bailey. Has anyone seen these damn spooks but you?"

He looked indignant. "Mr. Joe, you have seen what happened to that schematic."

"I did. And I repeat. Has anyone else seen these haunts besides yourself?"

Bailey drew a breath. "There's SUZN in collating. She said she saw David Packard phase through her ceiling and down thru her desk. He went through the floor."

"Did anybody see him on the next floor?"

"She's on the first floor."

I adjusted my hat a little more fiercely than necessary. "Okay, Mr. Bailey, we'll talk to her next."

"And then there was Bill Hewlitt," he added.

"Huh?"

"You know, Packard's partner. In Hewlitt—"

"I know, I know! What about him?"

"Well, he apparently came up through ground level, went through all the cubicles between him and the roof, and then went out of sight."

"More than one comp saw this?"

He nodded. "I've heard a few have. Didn't see him myself."

It made sense. If Packard was around, it wouldn't do to leave Hewlitt out.

But of course, they were Ops. What would they be doing down here in the Community? Ops didn't even know about the Community, for Gates' sake.

I let Bailey precede me inside. "Take me to where the action is."

"Sir?"

"To your office, Bailey. And then we'll check the rest of the joint. I wanna know why they favored you."

He feigned a deep breath. "I've wondered about that, too. Very well, Mr. Joe, and watch your step."

⇉–⇇

I grilled a batch of comps in the place and they seemed to have the same story. A good percentage of them had seen or heard one of these floating meemies, but most chalked it up to a holo advertising stunt or something. Most of the younger ones had no idea of who those spooks were supposed to be. I weep for the next generation.

"Well, I was doing my usual job, y'know, sourcing those kind of videos for my Op," said Susan. "I think, y'know, he's probably on the young, hormonal side, but I still get my credits for it, so what the hey?"

"You'd be surprised at the age ranges of Ops who do that, or their sex range," I said. "Go on, Miss Susan."

"Well, I was just uploadin' to beat the ever-lovin' band, Mr. Joe, though I didn't really want to get my hands in all that filthy stuff, an' all of a sudden this man, I have to call him that, comes down through the ceiling, if you can imagine that."

"Feet or head first?"

"Feet first." She paused. "If it was someone from accounting, he'd at least be nice enough to use a portal. And what with the office regulations we have around here, Mr. Joe, nobody of the opposite gender would be rude enough to go through the ceiling. Even if he wanted a date."

"I see. And what did he look like?"

"Well, he looked like a man. Like a man from the Community. Or like, I suppose, an Op, if you want to get technical. I mean, in a sense we are always getting technical here, but—"

"Miss Susan."

"Yes. Well, he looked quite distinguished. Like a gentleman. His shoes were very well taken care of. He had on a dark suit, very much a businessman's outfit, and a striped tie. And when I finally got to see his head, he was rather striking for an older gentleman. Bald on top, and what hair he had was white, but he had a friendly enough expression."

"Not threatening?"

"Well, not what I'd say threatening. I was just cringing against the collation device. I mean, well, really!"

"Please continue, Miss Susan."

"It didn't occur to me to speak to him. Well, I take that back. It did, but I really didn't want to. I just hoped he wouldn't notice me."

"Did he?"

She clasped her hands together over her knee, trying to conceal their shakiness. "Not that I could tell. Well, he just didn't turn his head my way, not that I wanted him to or anything. I was very glad he didn't stop in the room. Very glad. He just went through the floor, feet first, like he'd gone through the ceiling. The last thing I saw was the top of his bald head. And after it sank through the floor, I waited a couple of moments, and I just screamed! I mean, I screamed!"

"I understand, Miss Susan. What happened after that?"

"Well, Mr. REGI, who runs our department, ran in and asked me what was going on. I told him a man had just gone through the ceiling and the floor. In a straight line. He asked me who it looked like, and I told him it looked like a man. He asked me to be more specific. I mean, really. How many men just up and go through someone's ceiling and floor like that? I didn't ask for his infostrip!"

It was hard for me to suppress a chuckle. "Did anyone below you see this man?"

"They said nobody did. But you know how management is. They'd hush it up. They'd hush me up, too, but my scream drew a number of people. So they couldn't say it didn't happen."

"But they could say you were hallucinating?"

"Oh, yes. And they did."

"How did you know it was David Packard?"

"Well, I didn't. Not until I was having a break with that dear Mr. Bailey, and I told him about it. I described the man, you know? I have a way with descriptive words. So when I described him, Mr. Bailey went and got a history unit on our Op Forefathers, you know? And he brought up a page and showed me a .jpeg and asked if that was the man. I was stunned, simply stunned. I said, yes, it was, and he told me it was David Packard. I mean, my word! What would David Packard want with me?"

I shrugged. "I don't know what he'd want with anyone, Miss Susan. That's what I'm here to find out."

She rubbed her neck, thoughtfully. "Mr. Joe. Do you really think I had a hallucination?"

I slapped my notepad shut and put it in my pocket. "If you have, Miss Sally, so have a lot of other people. And we're going to learn why."

What the rest of it amounted to was talking to a bunch of people and getting their stories, the usual shamus stuff. Some had seen the ghosts, some hadn't. Several had been very impressed and tried to make contact, but the ghosts didn't pay any mind and kept sinking or rising. I noted for the record that the movement only seemed to be up or down, not horizontally. These ghosts would have made a lousy football team.

So I sat in Reggie's office with Bailey and gave him my report. Reg was built more like a traditional businessman, bulky, suited, black-haired, smoking a cigar that gave off virtual smoke and never had to be relit or have the ashes tipped off. "So," he said, drumming his hands on a blotter that changed colors continuously, "you think the building is haunted?"

"I don't know, Mr. Reggie," I said. "All I'm prepared to say is that you seem to be getting one hell of an historical floor show."

He winced. I wasn't facing Bailey. "I'd like to spend the night in Bailey's office," I said. "If any phenom comes my way, I'll have something to work with. That all right?"

He shrugged. "If you wish. This is coming out of Bailey's pocket, not mine." That time I looked, and Bailey did wince. He continued: "What do you propose to do if there really are ghosts here?"

Managing a sigh, I said, "Maybe grab a priest from First Gates. But first, I gotta see for myself what's going on here."

Bailey finally spoke up. "Mr. Joe. Do you feel there's a possibility that we may have been victimized by—by Woznians?"

"If we have, Mr. Bailey, I'll do my best to show them the way home."

⋛-⋚

The place usually ran 24/7 but they cleared it out just for me that night. I tromped up and down the halls, checked out the offices, rode the elevator up and down, thumped the walls, eyeballed security scans to make sure they were working. The only one in there besides myself was HeRB, the overnight security bot. He manifested as a hockey player. If that was how he cared to dress, okay.

"What's your take on it, Herb?" I asked, holding up a wall casually with my back.

"My take, man? My take?" Herb, outfitted in crew cut, goatee, and Red Wings jacket, couldn't wait for someone to ask. "Me, I think it's evidence of the Multicommunity."

"The Multicommunity?"

"Right, man, right. Like them Michael Rorschach novels, the ones with the Eternal Computerion in 'em. See, in his novels, there's a Digital Champion who can manifest himself in all realms when he's needed."

"Do tell."

Herb nodded, vigorously. "There's more than one level of Community out there, man. Some have a white-skinned computer who wields a nasty battle-axe that sucks programming. Others have a scanner imbedded in their forehead that can wipe their whole memory if it wakes up. Others..."

"I get the picture, Herb. Now, can you tell me how that relates to our present situation?"

He leaned over, conspiratorially. "There has to be a level between us and the Ops. And maybe, just maybe, when one of the Big Ops dies, one of the Pioneers, his soul goes there. Or it gets encoded, somehow. That makes sense, doesn't it?"

"ME, I THINK IT'S EVIDENCE OF THE MULTICOMMUNITY."

"Wouldn't want to deny it," I said.

"See, Michael Rorshach has the inside data. He's gotta. I mean, I always knew all those stories he wrote couldn't just have been made up. You ought to be talking to him, man."

"I'll make a note of it." Looking around, I said, "I wonder when the next Ghost Transit leaves. Gettin' tired of standing around."

"Oh, don't joke about that, man. I mean, speak of the Woz and..."

On cue, somebody came up from the floor.

Couldn't tell exactly who it was then, but I didn't have time to research. This time it was a lady, as I could guess from the hairdo as she started emerging from the floor. Her hair was light brown and she had it in a pretty elaborate 'do (as compared to, say, Alice, who goes for the quick and easy style), festooned with a big old golden headband that sported a fake gold rose. On the back of her head was a kind of bonnet with black silk flowers, gold medallions, and sashes trailing it that came down the front of her dress (as I saw when she emerged far enough). Her face was pale, her eyes large and dark, her nose fairly thin, her lips rouge red, and she looked very pretty.

Her dress appeared to be light blue, with dark blue flowers scattered over it. It reached all the way down to what would have been the floor for her, and she looked to be wearing a bustle. I registered all that and committed it to memory. I just hoped ghost Communitarians photographed.

The lady didn't seem to be looking at us. I ran forward and said, "Ma'am, a word, please. We need to talk." That didn't stop her from going upwards in her invisible elevator.

Behind me, Herb was yelling, "Arriup! Arriup! Skull and Bones for my Lord Arriup!" I figured I'd better 'arriup and see if I could catch her.

The levitating lady was already putting her cranium into the room above us. I had to hoof it to the stairs. Unlike her, I couldn't just rise to the occasion. Building walls in the Community had codes that made them solid as granite, or maybe ply-wall, to us. You only got through them when you were knocked through 'em.

Racing like a lame particle in a cyclotron, I got to the next floor just as her feet were about five inches from the floor. All depended on the next bit, which was to hurl myself forward and try to tackle her. My hands, arms, and chest made contact at about waist-height on our ghost girl.

They contacted nothing.

I felt a tingly sensation as I passed thru her and landed face-first on the floor. That sensation was something more than tingly.

The Immaterial Girl was still mostly in the room. I shoved myself back up and jumped at her, my hands flailing for her ankles, or at least the bottom of her skirt. No good, but my hands tingled more. I fell on my knees.

She drifted on up through the ceiling and I wasn't at an angle to look up her dress.

"Son of a Woz," I muttered, and tried to get to the next level. When I got to the stairs again, I reconsidered, loped to the elevator, got inside, and gave it the sign to get me to the next floor. Another maze of offices, but my quarry was still rising faster than the hopes of an Op on his 24th hour of World of Warmongers.

The important thing, to me, is that she wasn't doing anything. Not leaving a message or making a hand-sign or the like. No, it was just like she was doing her rounds on an inspection tour. If that was what she wanted, that was okay by me. But I wanted more input than that.

I kept going up by the elevator, a level at a time, and she continued her uninterrupted journey. Finally, we ended up on the roof. I got there just as her big gold medallions were showing up.

"Lady, please," I said, about a foot away from her. "I need to know what's going on. I'm a detective. You're in trouble? I can help. Let's talk."

But she didn't stop for a quick chat, or anything else. She kept rising until she was free of the building, and into the air, and very hard to make out, and then impossible to see. The phantom phenom had revealed itself.

I pushed my fedora on a little harder and rode the elevator back to the lobby. Herb was holding up a sheet of drawing-screen on which he'd crudely drawn eight radiating arms with suckers on them.

"The Eight Arms of Chaoctopus!" he chanted. "Arriup, Skull and Bones. Do not enwrap me in your tentacles."

I shoved him aside. "Herb, lemme see the data bank here."

He obliged. It was a small hookup behind the front desk. I put my hand in it, interfacing, and transmitted my images of the woman who rose through walls. In a moment, I had a match.

My eyes probably narrowed at what I saw on the screen. "Ada Lovelace," I read.

"Who?" Herb paused long enough in his chanting to ask.

"Ada Lovelace, born AD 1815, died AD 1852 by Op records. That's her."

"But, Joe, that's about a hundred years before the Community."

"And our Miss Ada, according to this, helped out Charles Babbage with his granddaddy analytical engine. She developed the first algorithm that could be used by a Communitarian. In short, she's one of our Founding Mothers."

Herb was in such awe he let down his octopus drawing. "Gosh. What are we gonna do?"

"Submit a report and see who turns up next."

⇒-⇐

From what I understand, Ops have a morning ritual called Breakfast. We don't have physical stuff you can put in your mouth and chew up. But we do have an Expander spinoff that helps burn off your fatigue and cleans up your memory cells, and we usually take that before the working day. We just call it Good Start.

So Alice and I were sitting in a booth across from each other in a Good Start place, a thumb and pinky apiece in a couple of plates on a table. It was great for getting things sorted out early on, and in case you wanted to do some face-to-face stuff, you couldn't beat it. About eleven other people were in the place, and we mutually ignored them.

"This has to be a first, Joe." Alice had manifested a chic 3-piece biz ensemble. "A real ghost story."

"Uh huh," I propped up my chin with the knuckles of my left hand. "And I'll be damned if I know where to start or stop on this thing."

"Come again?" She leaned in a bit closer, cleavage not in display but suggested nicely by the shirt and blazer.

"How do we prove these things are really ghosts?" I scratched my ear with my free hand. "If we do prove they are, how do we communicate with them?"

"Hold up a big sign that says STOP AND BE FRIENDLY."

"Alice, don't tell jokes for a living. Thirdly, what's their motivation? Why do a bunch of Pioneer big shots in their cyberplasm show up in that place at that time? None of them died there, and I don't see it as being a great vacation spot for the afterlife."

She shrugged. "That's why they've got guys like you for hire, Joe. Lucky for me."

"A couple of comps have already filed their resignations," I continued. "Most of the rest seem to be holding up okay. But Bailey seems to be the key, and I haven't figured out the...nope, I can't do a lock metaphor. He's the only one the spooks have spoken to."

"Plus he got that Eniac thing."

"He did. I don't specialize in chips-and-sorcery stories. But I'm gonna see what I can find out from another source."

Alice looked interested. "Who would that be?"

"Al, baby, I want you to make a call. Get me an appointment with the Church of Gates."

As far as Gates goes, let me say that I'm a semi-believer. I have seen too many folks crack their motherboards open with dissonant thinking to go all the way. But I would not label myself an atheist nor an agnostic, either. Too many times things have gone my way when they shouldn't, and if there is a Gates, I am not about to insult him by disbelieving. I can use a friend Up There.

But it had been a long time since I manifested myself into a pew. When I was newly assembled, I became a church member. My attendance became more sporadic and I lapsed soon enough. It wasn't so much that I had a problem with the Church as I had problems with work and life. Make of that what you will. I don't care.

Still, once Alice set me up, I zipped myself to the tall building with the funny windows depicting Our Founder in various stages of his journey. I remembered the old hymn, "He Will Meet Me in Silicon Valley," and hummed it to myself as I walked up to the doors.

I got about ten steps onto a floor with 1's and 0's set into the tiles when Brother PtrIK stepped out of an alcove and met me, hand outstretched. The echo effect they'd set up in this place had real style, and I wondered if I could approximate it someday. "Joe," he said, smiling. "It's been awhile."

Giving him back the smile, I shook his hand. "It has, Pat. Glad you still recognize me."

Pat wore a black robe, the traditional white cap with the bill facing backwards, and simulated Hush Puppies. I didn't know how long that fashion would last, but it seemed fitting for him. His face showed lines of dignity and he wore a hairline shot thru with grey and fading back to a widow's peak. I had no doubt it made his parishioners trust him.

"The way your mug gets changed every so often, boyo, I may not be able to do it much longer," he said. "Your secretary said you had a spiritual matter. Is that correct?"

"Got more spirits than I can handle," I concurred. "Not the kind that come out of an Expander, either. Where's your office?"

"This way." Pat led me thru a supposedly-solid wall into an office, from which a brown-backgrounded picture of Gates smiled down on us. Some cops kept small copies of it in their chest pockets. A few swore it had saved them from death.

The priest sat down at a simple desk, a few Gatesian verses on the wall (I scanned for anything from the Book of Mozilla, but none of that showed) and gestured me to sit down as well. "So. What's your pleasure, Joe?"

"Not much pleasure, Pat," I said, taking my hat off and fooling with it to give my hands something to do. "I'm investigating a haunted office building."

Pat's eyebrows looked like they could merge with his hairline just before they did. "What's the specifics, my boy?"

I downloaded what I knew. At the end, I asked, "So. What do you make of it?"

He sat there thinking, his left forefinger tapping his cheek. Finally, Pat said, "Quite frankly, Joe, I'm as bumfuzzled as you. Of course, we believe in holy Translation. That's the doctrine in which our core-selves are uploaded to the Great Server to live in peace. On the other hand, we have no specific doctrine dealing with ghosts."

Slapping my hat against my knee more or less rhythmically, I asked, "Does the church have any records of ghost sightings?"

Pat shrugged. "Some claim to have seen images they can't verify. All the way back to our many-tubed ancestors, or even abaci. A few even claim to have seen Ops."

I shuddered. Sure, I've seen scans of Ops. Every Communitarian has. But never have I seen an Op in the 3D, and I'm not sure I ever want to.

"What about...you know...contrary spirits?"

"Ah, you mean Woznians." Pat looked at the desk, and then at me. "Never encountered one and hope I don't. There are tales of such things, how they maddened Units until a Great Reboot was performed. Probably a lot of that was just viruses. About a few, I'm not really sure."

"Did you ever meet somebody who'd done a Great Reboot?"

"Yeah. He wasn't pretty." Pat fixed me with a glance. "Joe. He datawiped himself."

I sat stock still. Suicide?

"Never thought a priest would do something like that," I said, finally.

"Don't think that we're a different breed of Comp than you, Joe. Some of us have to take on jobs as dangerous as any Ring agent. Sometimes, we... no, I can't talk about that. But, Gates help us, we can break too."

"So what's your advice, Pat?"

"My advice is, you go back there tonight. And you take me with you."

>-<-

Our favorite ghost spa was getting used to my presence by now, but Pat the priest was a new code patch, so to speak. When we walked in the door, people stopped and stared for an instant, then smiled and came forward to press the pixels with Pat. My pal doled out a few blessings. Herb was still on duty and quickly held up a screenshot of the third floor to hide the octopus on his chest.

Pat was amused. "It's okay, my son. I've read a few of his books too."

Herb gasped in relief. "That's great, father, which ones?"

"Later." Pat was no more eager to deal with geeks than I was. We took the elevator up to Reggie's office and the manager was out of his chair like a politician looking for a handout. His hand was out, too, and it pumped Pat's.

"Mr. Patrick," he said, smiling almost in 360 degrees. "I'm so glad to have you here in our construction."

"Thank you, Mr. Reggie," Pat smiled, "and I hope to see you in mine as well."

I saw Reggie's smile flicker a little less for a second. Then it turned back on. "Yes. Well, we'll do the usual shutdown for you while you're here tonight. And Mr. Joe, of course."

"Of course," I muttered, pushing my fedora back a notch.

"Everybody but Herb will be out of the building," said Reggie. "And if you want, we can send him home, too."

"Actually, Reggie, there's one more I'd like to have stay with us."

"Who?"

"Bailey."

Reggie's pop-eyes widened so far the conjunctiva could have been seen a hundred meters away. "Him? Oh, no, no. Out of the question."

"Why?" Pat was standing beside me, arms folded.

"Because he doesn't want to!"

"Why would that be?" I let Pat do his strong silent type. It was working.

"Because, because he's frightened. He thinks there are Woznians about."

"And if there are," Pat placed his valise on Reggie's desk, "I'm loaded."

Reggie looked from one of us to the other repeatedly, faster than REM movement. I had to admit, it amused me. The powerful always look humorous once they realize they've reached the limit of their power.

"You could deny us," I put in. "But if you do, both of us will walk away and you can go back to your haunted hacienda."

"Well, now, that's not, not very funny," blustered Reggie.

"It's not meant to be," said Pat, getting back in the game. I was glad he didn't have me in his confessional.

Finally, Reggie settled back in his chair with a big fake whoosh of pseudobreath. He was miming Op behavior, I guess, but neither one of us cared. "All right. I'll ask him to stay tonight."

"We'll ask him to stay tonight," I said.

>-<

That night, the priest and I sat in Bailey's office at two desks opposite Bailey's, with Bailey himself occupying desk number three. He had the jitters, which I did not begrudge him. After all, he was the only one who'd heard anything as well as seen it.

At present, he was finger-sucking at a portable Expander. It wasn't at full strength, but he probably needed the comfort.

Pat walked over and put a hand on his shoulder. "Rest easy, Mr. Bailey. You've got Joe to handle the physical and me to handle the spiritual. If there is any of that."

Bailey gave him a sour smile. "Oh, it's there all right, Father Pat. I've heard them. I saw their sign."

"The inverted schematic of Eniac," I clarified for Pat.

"That," said Bailey, pretty much flatly. I didn't blame him.

I adjusted myself in the seat, my feet still on the desktop. "Look, Mr. Bailey. I don't know much from sorcery. But I do have a proclivity for following up clues. Got some questions I want to ask you, some of which I've asked before, some not. But I want you to answer them all. Okay?"

Bailey nodded. Pat looked serious.

"One: who have you done badly enough to make them want to mess with you?"

"I, I haven't," he said.

"Think hard, Mr. Bailey. Everyone has enemies, known to them or not."

He mimicked a swallow. "I'm not sure. Does anybody want my office?"

"Do they?"

"I don't know!"

"Mr. Bailey, someone or something has targeted you. I don't know

"THE INVERTED SCHEMATIC OF ENIAC."

anyone else who has heard these voices of Babbage, including me. I don't know anybody who was sent a copy of the Eniac thing. I don't know..."

"Wait." Pat held up his hand. "The insides of Eniac. Where would someone get that?"

I'm sure my eyes widened.

"Not too many places," I answered. "And believe it, not too many access points. We need an All Community Bulletin on this."

"Yes," Pat agreed. "But in the morning. For now, we sit and wait."

After awhile, Bailey spoke.

"I'm sure everyone has some enemies."

Pat and I waited.

"There was a girl I once linked to," Bailey continued wistfully. "She wanted to make it a permanent connection. But there was another one I was trying for, and..." His voice faded away.

"So what happened to choice number 0 and choice number 1?" I asked.

He looked down. "The first one cursed me and left in tears. The second one I never got. To this day, I am unconnected."

Pat said, rather gently, "You said she cursed you. In what way, Mr. Bailey?"

"Oh, just the generic way. 'Damn your data and your core, erase you five thousand times and one more, go to the pits of Woz and never find your way out.'"

Kind of medium for cussing, I thought. I'd put up with phrases thrown my way that would sizzle the motherboard of a Cray.

"What became of her after that?" asked Pat.

"I never saw her again."

"Now, why does that not surprise me?" I muttered.

Pat gave me an unkind look. But before he could reprimand me, the floor show started happening.

Or to be more precise, the from-under-the-floor show began.

At one time, the tops of three heads protruded from the tiling. They were shortly followed by three business-suited Op ghosts, all male, probably from the most recent Founding era. I couldn't ID them offhand, but it didn't seem to matter.

There were more emerging, as those three hit chest level.

I heard a shriek behind me. When I pivoted, Bailey was making for the elevator. Really, I couldn't blame him. But I hollered, "Hold on, you're safer here with us!"

Didn't matter. He got the doors open, got them closed, and vamoosed.

More and more Founding Oppers were coming through the floor and leaving thru the ceiling. They practically filled the room. Pat had his Omega symbol out and looked about as savage as I'd ever seen him. "By the power of Gates, I resist you! By the power of Gates, I cast you out!"

Honestly, it didn't stop them any more than a low-power shield stops a logic bomb.

Now, there was some chanting, though I never saw any of the Op ghosts open his or her mouth. It mostly was one word:

BABBAGE...BABBAGE...BABBAGE...BABBAGE...

This was getting creepier than a tale of a haunted housing. No, it'd passed that creep level a long time ago.

What the hell could I do?

I launched myself forward, arms out first, and pushed my face into the face of an emerging Op.

Oh, Gates.

I really shouldn't have done that.

"Joe. Joe. Can you hear me? Joe, are you tracking? Joe, talk to me."

The voice was familiar and I pulled its vocalist out of my memory bank. Darkness began giving way to light. I reached out and grabbed a cloak. Two hands grabbed my wrists.

"Pat," I said. "Oh, Pat."

The priest's face began to materialize before me. Sensors kicked in, reluctantly, and I saw Pat's face the way I'd seen it a few times before: in deep concern.

"It's me, Joe," he confirmed. "Can you let go of my cloak?"

I forced my hands open. He eased up his grip. "How do you feel, Joe?"

"How do I feel?" I said, and repeated it with emphasis: "How do I feel?"

"Yeah. How?"

My senses were firming up and I saw the room about us. I must have kicked over some stuff, including the desk nearest me. For starters, I was lying on my back and Pat was bending over me. I sensed someone else in the room. Didn't have the vantage point or strength to track him.

"I'll tell you when I know," I replied at last.

Pat made a face. "Give, Joe. Tell me what happened."

"I don't want to," I muttered.

"I don't give a delete what you want! Talk!"

Sighing, I lay back and let the tiles massage me. "You know what's below even negative numbers, Pat?"

"Have a feeling you can tell me," his grip was gentler.

"Shoved my face into that Pioneer's face and I was in the Data Pit."

He flinched.

I went on. "Don't ask me how it was, I don't retain a lot. My systems probably dumped the info. Self-protection."

Pat nodded. "What can you say?"

"I can say it was as close to damnation as I ever wanna get. Ever."

Another voice said, "So you think it's legitimate haunting?"

That was Reggie. He came close enough so that I could see him from my point of view. For once, he looked like he gave a damn about me.

"Don't know. Never been haunted before."

Reggie turned towards Pat. "What's your opinion, father?"

Pat said, "I haven't formed one yet. Those things didn't seem to be fazed by the Omega, or anything else I brought up. And I brought up a lot."

"They're that tough?" The manager looked very concerned.

"Nothing's that tough," Pat declared.

He moved tentatively, from one foot to the other. "Gentlemen, as far as I'm concerned, you've earned your credits. I'll move operations from this building to another. I appreciate your efforts and we can wrap this up."

"No," I said. "We can't."

Both of them looked at me with a look the Disk Doctor gives to cases beyond repair.

I pushed myself up to a sitting position, mostly. "Look. I don't know what I went through there, and I don't want to go through it again. But we haven't settled anything here. Still don't know who or what these haunts are, or what they want. That's an unfinished job. I don't do that kind of work."

The priest kept silent, but he looked encouraged. Reggie looked dubious. "You really want to go through that again?"

"Of course not. Like the priest said, I don't give a delete what I want. It's what I've gotta do."

After a pause, Reggie asked, "Why do you have to do it, Mr. Joe?"

After a pause of my own, I answered, "Because not even Woz can keep me from finishing a case."

>-<

The next day, I took off. That is, I stayed on the office couch with Alice massaging my shoulders. It felt good.

"Want to tell me some of your traumatic experience?" she inquired.

"Honey, I don't even want to tell me about that experience."

"Was it worse than that trip Henry put you through?"

I sighed. "Alice, Henry's trip was about expanding your mind in ways you never thought possible. When I stuck my face into that ghost—"

"Yes?"

"It expanded it into things I never wanted to believe were possible."

She kept up the massage. "Do you think your mind is all right?"

"Yeah, yeah. So far as I can tell. Pat prayed for me and gave me a Resistance medal."

"And you feel better with them?"

"Believe it. I do." I sighed. "But I'm not giving up the case. I just can't. It's a job. I never slack off on a job."

Alice kept the healing touch going, silently, for a few seconds.

"You know what I love about you?"

"I don't even know why my motherboard loves me."

She giggled, but didn't lose rhythm. "Because you really are a paladin, Joe."

I did a quick reference. "You think I'm like a guy from an old TV western on YouTube?"

Alice slapped me between the shoulder-blades. "Don't be a vacuum. I know you. You, Joe, will go out and do this one not just for Mr. Bailey or Mr. Reggie or father Patrick, but because of the principle."

"Yeah, Alice. I'm very principled. And my gullibility quotient is rated almost as high as your looks."

"Flatterer."

"It's true. How long has it been since you linked?"

"None of your enterprise," she pinched me hard on the side. "Still, I am going to tell you something about yourself and you're gonna shut up and listen."

"All—"

"I said shut up!" She smacked me on the back of the neck. I stayed quiet. When she knew I was going to keep that way, she continued.

"You've put yourself online bad in two times that I know of, and probably a lot more that I don't. The first time, even Norton had a tough time putting you back together. Nobody would've blamed you if you had turned down any more assignments from the Ring. But you went charging back in, getting into that business with Henry, and came out chips intact. There's a reason they hire you for things like that, Joe. Not just because you'll get the job done. But because you've got a heart. And."

She stayed silent so long I ventured a word. "And?"

"And you wouldn't be able to live with yourself if you didn't. How about that?"

I shrugged. "Your diagnosis has got some merit, Al. I gotta admit. I should tell you about yourself sometime."

"Turn over."

I did. She had demanifested her clothes.

Before I could say anything, she took my head between her hands. "How long has it been, Joe? Doesn't matter."

Then she kissed me and we cut to the fireplace.

>-<

The Temple of Wozniak was not intended to be found easily. It took a lot of research on my part and arguing with Father Pat to get me a lead on it. Nonetheless, I found my way there. Having done so, I wondered why in the hell I had.

It was a three-story edifice done up all in black...more like a black that reached 180 shades beyond normal black. There's no way I can communicate that and no reason why I should. The angles of the exterior defied normal geometrics and probably a number of natural laws. You didn't get in without an appointment. Pat had to be noodged and he had to noodge someone in government that he knew. Suppose I could have called the Ring, but after my last two jobs with them, I'd rather they called me first.

The front door looked something like a mouth. That's all I'll say. I was scanned at the door and it opened. But not outward or inward. Nope, this one retracted from a break in the middle, going up at the top and down at the bottom.

Like a mouth.

I stepped inside and replayed verses from The Old and New Contracts in my memory.

A joker who was manifesting more arcane symbols on his body than I ever knew existed batted long black eyelashes at me. "Identify," he said.

"Say please," I said.

When he started to scoff, I got up in his space and looked down at him, meaningfully. "Please," he said.

"My name's Joe. I have an appointment here. Buzz me in."

He said nothing, but nodded for me to follow, and I did. On the walls were posters that looked like recruiting gambits for the Pit. I liked the one best that had a staring Woz pointing out with the legend, HE WANTS YOU.

The flunky ushered me into the office of someone who was probably Father Pat's opposite number. "Low one, Mr. Joe is here."

"Send him. In," said a voice trying too hard to be scary.

With a gesture, the go-between guy admitted me into the unholy of unholies.

Really, it was mostly an office. That is, if offices featured pictures of an upside-down Gates in agony, pierced thru the gut with something metallic and fearsome, and a very, very shadowy portrait of Wozniak himself. There were a few unimportant nicknacks on the desk before me, including a trophy for online golf. That, somehow, was reassuring.

The character in the chair behind the desk was not. He was too theatrical.

His head was mostly bald, with a couple of ridges of hair coming from the back, circling over his dome, and ending pretty near his eyes. Said eyes had blackened lids and came with catlike pupils. His nose was long enough to be impressive and he wore his mustache and goatee long. The robe he wore was blood-red (as far as I can tell from research) and had fanged mouths in various places. His fingernails were long, and on his left ring finger he had a golden ring with some kind of symbol on it of which I wasn't hot on learning the meaning.

He smiled and showed pointy teeth. "I am Brother Undertow. How may I help you, Mr. Joe?"

I occupied a chair in front of his desk. "Just looking for some info on a case, thanks. Thought you might be able to help with some research."

His eyebrows rose, making an interesting pattern with those two ridges of hairs. "Of the haunted edifice?"

"Guess word gets around."

He did an open-hand gesture that didn't seem too diabolical. "Details?"

I gave him the gist of the apparition appearances. The proceedings seemed interesting to him, gauging by his expression.

"So," I said. "What do you think?"

Brother Undertow waited for a long moment before saying, "I don't know what to think."

I leaned in closer. "Let's do a little better than that, shall we?"

Undertow shrugged. "There are tales of Wozniak manifesting, blessed be his designation. However...the spirits of Pioneers? Dead Pioneers?"

My arms were crossed and I stayed silent. He was going to have to do the heavy lifting.

"Really, never heard of such a thing," he said, at last.

"What about the upside-down Eniac?"

"Ah, well," he sighed. "Symbolic, I suppose. But, again, that's not a phenomenon I'm familiar with."

"Which means it hasn't happened before."

"Correct." This time, he let me be the first to answer.

"But that doesn't mean it couldn't be happening for the first time."

"No. It doesn't."

"To your mind, what would make it a true manifestation of...you know?"

He rubbed his ring, thoughtfully. "Actually, Mr. Joe...may I call you Joe?"

"Mr. Joe is just fine."

"Well, then, Mr. Joe, I cannot rule it out but I cannot rule for it. As told in our manifests, when the Contradictor was cast out of the Silicon Valley, he showed himself to a few, operated through others, but...he was not absent from the showings."

"Meaning he liked to make appearances?"

"If that's how you want to put it," affirmed Undertow.

"So given that he hasn't made an appearance, it's not likely he's involved."

"Mr. Joe," Undertow leaned forward giving me a look I didn't like, "he is always involved. But directtly? In this instance? I cannot rule one nor zero."

I decided I'd spent time enough there. "Thanks for your cooperation, sir. See you around."

"Mr. Joe, I might see those phenomena myself, if you wished."

"I don't think Father Pat would like that."

Couldn't get out of there fast enough. On the way out, I heard strains of "Sympathy For the Woz."

I dampened my hearing till I was far away from there.

>-<

Luckily, Father Pat was around with a couple of warm Expanders.

"I'm on the housing of it, but not in the meat," I complained.

Pat nodded, sagely. "I ought to be more knowing of this business than

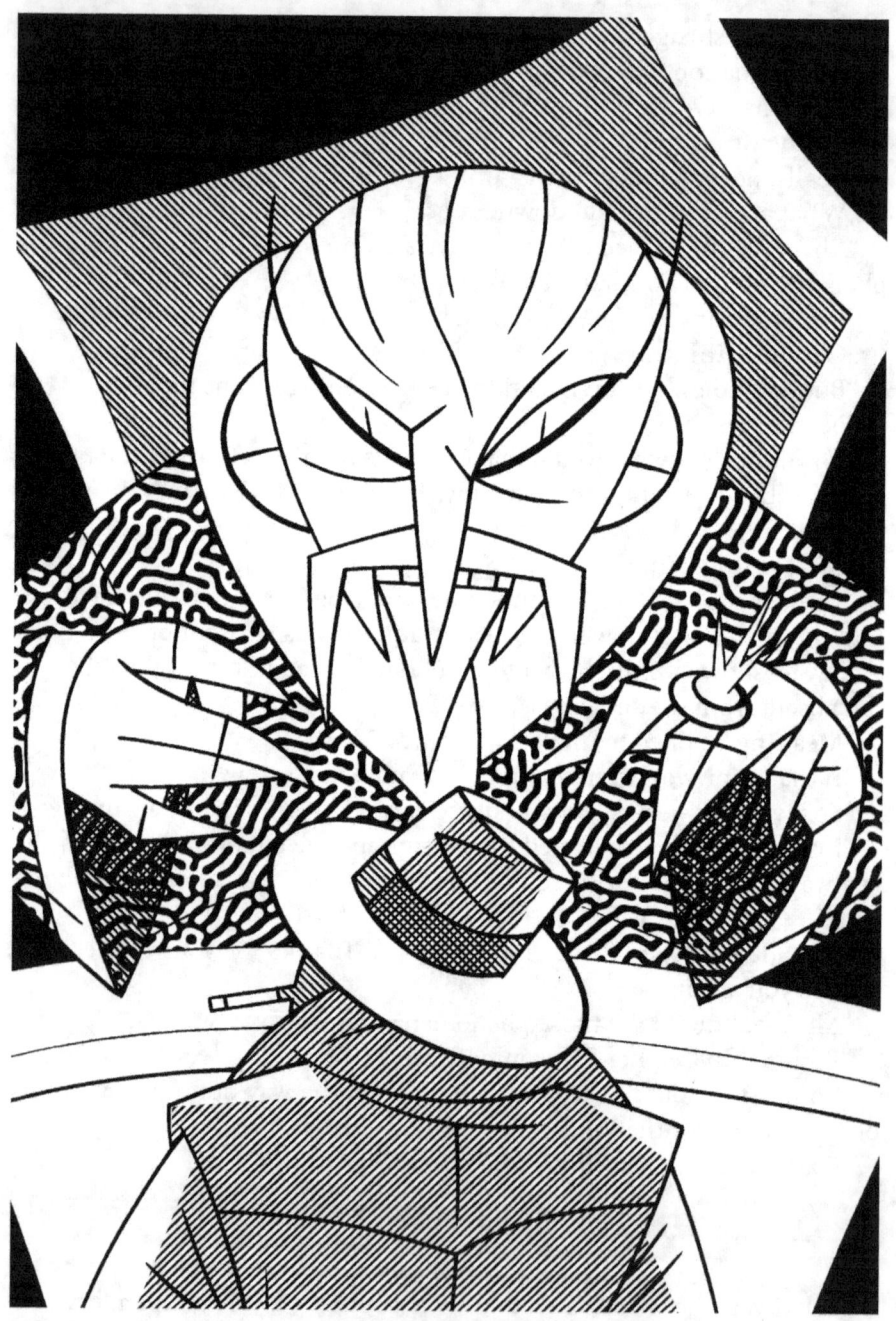

"BUT, AGAIN, THAT'S NOT A PHENOMENON I'M FAMILIAR WITH."

you, Joe, but I'm stupefied this time, too."

"Ghosts," I sniffed hard. "I have enough trouble with cyberthugs and crooks. Why ghosts? What makes me think I can track down ghosts?"

"Maybe because you're so good at your other cases. I don't know all the details, but trust me, you've got a rep."

"And here I stand in great chance of blowing it, all because I can't figure out why this guy Bailey is getting the spook treatment." I took my hand out of the Expander and put both hands in my hair. "Why Bailey? Why him?"

"Indeed," Pat agreed. "Why him? Or is it really about him?"

I fixed Pat with a cool stare. "Are you giving me an insight, Pat?"

He shrugged like Atlas. "Nothing more than what I've learned in the confessional pod. Sometimes you have to hit around a thing before you figure out where the real target is."

For once in a long time, the relays started working in my mind. "I think you've got a lead. Got a plug in here to the city records database?"

"Sure," he brought over a terminal. "Know what you're looking for?"

"Not yet," I admitted, getting my hands on its surface. "But maybe soon. Very, very soon."

᠈-᠈

After my paw-through of the city records, I contacted Bailey. He was in his office and looking paler than the inside of a potato. "I'm glad you've come," he rasped. "But it may be too late. They're closing the building down. Closing down the company."

I sat across from him and leaned forward. "Now, why would they want to do that, Bailey?"

He moistened his lips. "Because no one wants to work in a spectrally infestated locale."

"You mean, in a haunted building."

"Well, yes."

I leaned back and grabbed my knee in both hands. "If I'm right, Bailey, and I think I am, that just may not be a problem."

He blinked. "How do you mean, Mr. Joe?"

"I mean, I want to get you, Father Pat, Susan, and Reggie all in the same room at the same time. Heck, I might even get Herb in here for the fun of it. Wouldn't that be something?"

"I, I don't know what it'd be."

Getting up, I said, "I've got a good idea, Bailey. We all just might like it. Except for one, of course."

"Who?"

I just smiled and went out.

>-<

A day later, I had the aforementioned group assembled in the building's meeting room. I won't comment on the décor, but I'm glad I didn't work there.

I had Reggie lock the door and I stood between everyone else and it. Didn't want anybody lamming out while I was playing my part as the big investigator in the big revelation scene.

"I'm glad you all came," I began, "because I think I've finally figured this one out."

Father Pat and I gave Bailey, Susan, and Reggie the eye. Bailey, as ever, looked nervous. Susan kept quiet. Reggie was stoic but not pleased.

"So, here's what I dug up. So far, spooks have been manifesting in your building. Through the basement, up past the roof, and beyond. Why? I doubt this place has been cursed. Probably a few disgruntled employees, but every business has those."

"It has to be," said Bailey. "It just has to be."

"Go ahead, Joe," Pat prompted. "We're ready for the floor show."

"Not if things come through the floor," said Susan.

I smiled. "Not much chance of that. Anyway, here's the play. Bailey came to me, said he'd heard things in his dreams. Said spirits had spoken to him. Audibly."

"They have," Bailey nodded.

"Bailey, please. We also have the evidence of the inverted schematics of Eniac. Also, every one of us has seen the ghosts. But none of us has heard them talk. Except Bailey."

Dead silence.

"Every time we came to observe the spooks, Bailey has hung behind."

"I was scared!" Bailey piped up.

"Don't blame you. But consider this. Father Pat's exorcism didn't work. I'm not saying he's flawless, but you'd think even a benign spirit would have problems with that. And when I talked with Brother Undertow—"

Three of my guests flinched at the name. Father Pat just looked grim.

"—he told me that there was no manifestation of Woz-spirits that Woz himself had not appeared in. Guess what? In the cast members of all our spirits...Woz isn't included."

"Wish you'd quit saying that name," Susan groused.

"Sorry, ma'am," I told her.

"You did," said Bailey, "stick your face into Hell."

"I sure as hell did. At least, it sure as hell seemed like it. Never want to experience that again. But I got to thinking, and reexamining it, as little as I wanted to."

"And?" queried Father Pat.

"And I cross-referenced it with stuff from the Op world, info we deal with. Like Gustave Dore's illustrations of Dante's Inferno. Or Bosch's weirdo paintings. Or...but I could go on. The problem was, they matched up too well. Sure, they were in 3D, not 2D like the originals. But you could see the basis. This was animated Op stuff. Nothing original. A big, fat fake."

I let that sink in for a few seconds before I went on to the next point.

"Now, a couple of other things. The only time I actually heard those spooks speaking was when they were hollering 'Babbage'. I've got a recording capacity—hey, who doesn't?—and I played that back at a voice lab. There were a few people to match it up to. One of them was a really, really good match."

Silence.

That was fine by me. The voice lab belonged to the Ring.

"That one," I said, "was to this man."

I pointed at Bailey.

All eyes were on him, and his eyes indicated he was going apoplectic.

"What are you—why, I—" he spluttered.

"Yeah. You hired me. But that's one of the oldest gags in the data bank. You hired me to keep the heat off yourself."

"That's insane!"

"It's anything but insane. Grab him. Frisk him."

About the time Pat and Reggie went for him, the room filled up with ghosts.

There were ghosts by the megagross, Pioneers and Semipioneers and, yes, the return of the idiots from Dore and Bosch. You couldn't see through them, and none of us regular comps could see each other. But I closed my eyes and flailed away. "This is Joe!" I yelled. "Yell out your name!"

"Patrick."

"Reggie!"

"Sus—oomph!"

"Sorry," I kept flailing with arms and legs until, finally, I connected with something that wasn't wall, table, or chair.

At that point, the ghosts faded out. Everybody else came back into view. Susan was sitting on the floor, holding her shoulder where I'd hit it.

Lying on the floor not far from her, flat on his back, with a bruised jaw but still conscious, was Bailey.

I stood next to him with arms folded. "Want to show it to us? Or do I have to punch you again and take it off you?"

Looking at me with 10 GBs of hate in each eye, Bailey reached behind himself, pulled out a disk, and threw it at me. I caught it.

"A data projection disk!" Reggie exclaimed. "Been a long time since I've seen one of those."

"Yeah," I said. "Stuffed, no doubt, with animations of the Pioneers, of the oogy-boogies, and, probably, with the pictures of the guts of Eniac."

"And the sound recordings of voices saying 'Babbage'," added Pat.

"Which was Bailey's own, multiplied many, many times over." I paused.

"Bailey," Susan, now on her feet, "how could you?"

Pat smiled. "You may as well go ahead with your speech, Joe. We're all waiting."

"I'm not," muttered Bailey.

"Oh, yes you are. It took a little cogitation, but once we got the thread, it was easy to follow it up. And you gave me the clue yourself, Bailey."

He looked at me, not saying anything.

"You mentioned there was another girl you'd been trying for, but you couldn't get her. I wondered who it was. Asked around. Wasn't hard to find out."

Susan's eyes widened beyond what they should have been capable of.

"That's right, Miss Susan, he tried to ask you out a couple of times, did he not?"

"Well, yes. But really, I, I wasn't interested. I didn't think you'd make such a big deal about it, Bailey."

He glared at her with twice the venom he used on me.

"Some guys never show it," I went on. "They let it amplify inside themselves, throwing in a bunch of resistors to strengthen it. Then—pow! It escapes in one big spark."

Patrick looked at Susan, then at Bailey. But he kept silent.

"And if I'm right," I finished, "Susan found someone else she interfaced with better than Bailey. Isn't that right?"

Susan's mouth was open. I looked at Reggie. He was trying to talk, too. Then he just looked away.

"So, we've got a neat little motive there. Fill the building with enough ghosts and monsters, so that the firm has to abandon it, and probably Reggie, too. Maybe he hoped it'd break you two up. I dunno. But it was a strike at both of you, and that was his objective."

Patrick knelt down beside Bailey. "Better confess, son. It's always easier when you do."

He shook his head. "Call the Cops."

So we did.

⇒-⇐

It was obvious I wasn't going to get any credits from Bailey voluntarily on this one, but a friend in the Ring got in touch with a Judiciator and he got the bank to pry the money out of Bailey's account. Plus a tidy bonus for the effort I'd so nobly put in.

Reggie kicked in with a few credits, as well, and invited me to the wedding of Susan and himself later on that week. I thanked him but begged off.

I thanked Father Pat, too, and promised I'd be on time for a few sermons, even if I had to tune them in remotely. That promise I kept.

And that was the end of it.

Almost.

⇒-⇐

A week later, I was lying on the office couch, glad that we had enough cushion, both literally and monetarily, to ride things out. I studiously observe the right to be lazy in between cases, and I was observing like crazy.

Alice, trim and neat as the efficient secretary and love interest should be, burst in with an email in hand. "Joe, I think you better see this."

"Okay," I swung my feet to the floor.

"But maybe, maybe not," she said, clutching it to her chest.

"Alice, give it here."

She relented and handed it over. I took it and scanned it while sitting on the couch.

It read:

Mister Joe:

Thank you for your visit, and for notifying us of the pretender. It should serve as an example of the Uninitiated trying to meddle where they have no business. If you wish to become better acquainted with the faith, simply bring this letter with you on your next visit. We welcome men of your caliber.

Brother Undertow

And there was an attachment to it.

It was a news item with a picture of Bailey in it, and a report that he'd committed suicide in his cell. At least, they think it was suicide.

Really, he just looked very scared.

I gave the note back to Alice. "Nuke it," I said.

She deleted it as thoroughly as possible.

Any further ghostbusting cases will be referred to Father Pat.

THE COMPNAPPING
OF ALICE

It took me a good while to get out of sleep mode that Tuesday morning, and I didn't want to. When I awoke, the clanging of a million alarms in my head told me I should never have spent that much time Expanding at the bar last night. The hangover in my head was challenging every other one I'd ever had, and they weren't even on the graph with this one.

Getting up and manifesting myself some dress, I flushed myself of some of the Expansion—enough is enough, already—and took stock of my bedroom. In appearance, it probably wasn't any more impressive than an Op bedroom, from the .jpegs I've seen. Just a decent bed, a comlink on the wall beside it, a closet for my garment manifestations, a viewscreen on the wall in front of my bed so I could view the vicinity, and a portal to the rest of the house. I built it myself but I had to make payments on the cyberspace.

I shook my head to level down some more of the clanging, which was a major mistake. Had to go, no, sprint to the voidroom and get rid of more Expansies. Never again, at least until next week.

"Joe," I said to the reflecting screen before me, "you are one lousy looking matrixhumper."

But it was a work day. I did some face manipulation to make myself look more decent, and decided I'd take the Comlink to work. It'd cost more than public translation, but the little quartz clock was ticking. It took me a little time to put my hand on the wall plate and interface, but I did it.

I just hoped I wouldn't throw up on the way.

When I arrived at the office, which was the other virtual residence sucking credits out of my account, I whumped thru the wall plate there and the place was as it should be. Same desk with the pseudo oak finish, same comlinks (three of them in a row, on the wall), same emergencycache of replenishments and pick-me-ups in the box in the corner. Against the wall I had manifested a vintage 1970's record player and my music was on virtual disks because I wanted it that way. Maybe some old time stuff like Walter Carlos would cheer me up. I threw my hat on a hook and keyed my way thru the door to the outside office.

"Alice, I'm in," I started to say. I'm not sure what syllable I stopped on.

There was nobody in the outer office.

The desk of phony mahogany was there. The comlinks were within reach. The refreshment disks for our clients were stacked on the right side of the desk. The pics of Alice's heroes, mostly romance writers, were on one wall and the one opposite it displayed mine, which were mostly the virtsports aces I'd grown up with. And, yeah, the front door was still there, though nobody was ringing for admittance.

But no Alice.

I think I swore, but was careful not to use Woz's whole name. Since the incident with the Church I was more superstitious. Alice was always there before me. Even if we'd been out the night before, partying or on a case, with two hours to go before work-time, she preceded me. That woman worked like a Cray, and considering some of my habits, that wasn't such a bad thing to do.

She should've been there. Blonde, bouncy, long-legged, with a face to shame Helen of Troy (if anybody'd uploaded a .jpeg or .gif of Helen, instead of just a representation), with a backside that'd make an Op want to join the Community. That Alice. The one who knew just how to arrange her manifestation to make me glad I had a male plug.

Alice wasn't there.

I went to the comlink and connected to her place. Before the pixels could line up, I said, "Alice, this is Joe. Where are you, baby? The office is open and you aren't in it."

The viewscreen had her home manifested before I'd finished talking. Nobody was in it, not that I could see. I shifted the view all around, to display every room, every niche. I'd long since had permission from her to do this, and she with me.

The same pink and beige walls, the same romance and rom-comp disks, the voidroom that was a lot more organized than mine would ever be. The closet full of apparel suitable for office work, disguise duty, and a few more intimate situations. I guilt-tripped a bit for my snooping, but not very much.

No Alice.

I activated the Comlink for another budget-busting transmission. Before I went, I popped a call to the Ring. "Kelly, this is Joe," I said. "My secretary's missing. I can use all the help you've got."

Then I transmitted.

>-<

Kelly was in the house before me. Ring privileges.

"How are you, Joe? Never mind, I can imagine." He stuck his hand out and shook it. Kelly, real name KLEEE, was my best friend in the Big Ring. He manifested himself as an Op fifty-something, with grey hair at the temples and brown hair further up on the sides, thinning to almost nothing at the top. His eyes were greyer than his temple hairs, he had a nose that looked sharp as a dagger, and he was about 6 foot 1 in American measurements. I'd never seen him anywhere without his black business suit and white turtleneck.

"Thanks, Kelly. Appreciate you making time for me."

"Speaking of time," he said, "let's not waste it. How about the wall plate?"

"Glad you reminded me," I tried to make it sound like a joke. "Let's share a glare."

We went to the place on her pink wall where the plate was, right next to a big blowup of a romance novel cover. It featured a he and a she entwined, and the title in cursive below it: LOVE'S TENDER BYTES. This, I did not need at the moment. I put my hand against the plate and let it read me.

The image of us looking at the wall and the room behind us firmed up on the viewscreen. I turned my hand so that it would run backwards. It did so, and nothing much happened. I hyped the speed and when it came to 2 hours and 19 minutes back, the screen went solid black.

"Son of a W…" I started.

Kelly put his hand on my shoulder. "Find out how far back the interruption goes."

The damned darkness was a few hours long, though we covered it in about five minutes. The screen came up with a pic of Alice in the room, with her blue nightdress on, not looking at the plate. Since it was going backwards, I caught a glimpse of her with nothing on but her best intentions, and then one of her materializing the outfit she wore when we went out. A red blazer, a yellow blouse, a plaid skirt cut just above the knee, and pseudoleather boots. And that blonde, blonde hair.

Alice.

"Back a little further, Joe," Kelly advised.

I cursed but I don't remember what I said. Just as well. The playback continued in reverse, fast but not as quickly as when I had been paging thru the blackness. It showed her walking backwards, the door opening, me giving her a goodnight kiss that Kelly had no business seeing, then both of us backing through the door, which closed behind us. Or in front of us. What the hell.

We ran thru the imagery backwards, seeing a perfectly boring few hours with nobody in the place, then Alice backing thru the door, unmanifesting her dress, a moment of nudity, then emerging from the voidroom with her best face creation. She backed out of there with her makeup coming off and went back to bed.

I went thru the whole sleep time she had, backwards, until she got out of bed and manifested another nightgown, green this time. I froze the display.

"Did you catch anything I didn't?" Kelly asked. "Because I didn't."

Shaking my head, I said, "Not a damned thing. I'll run it forward, play with it awhile, but I don't think we're gonna find much. This looks like the work of a pro. A pro's pro."

Kelly nodded. "I'll dupe it and have our boys look at it, too. But I have my doubts we'll get much more than you do on your own."

I sat down on the floor, under the plate, the wall against my back, and rested my arms on my knees. "Which leaves us with: who took Alice, why, and where is she right now?"

He gave me the silent gaze with those piercing gray eyes. Both of us had to be thinking about the same thing. If we were lucky, Alice had just been compnapped. If not, she might have been crashed.

Crashing is, to put it in Op terms, as close as we can get to human murder. It is a forcible destruction of identity, memory, intelligence, everything that makes a comp a comp. Possibly the victim can be reprogrammed with other data, but the being that was is gone. It's not easy to do. But it can be done.

A crashed Alice was not the imagery I cared to put in my data bank.

I sighed. "I'm going on the basis that Alice is out there somewhere. I'm gonna find her. I'll find her if it takes till my fifth Op is dead."

Kelly nodded, silently.

"I'm going to need help, Kelly. Need the whole Ring."

He paused. "I'm afraid we can't, Joe."

"You what?" I sprang up and had his lapels in my hands before I knew I'd done so. "You can't?"

Kelly removed my paws gently, with a strength that belied his appearance. "I said we can't, Joe. Didn't say we wouldn't."

The hot-spot anger was replaced by bewilderment. "You better input that at a speed I can handle, Kelly. I'm not processing that worth a damn."

"This isn't Ring business, Joe. You know what level of things we deal with. The whereabouts of your secretary, even given your primo service, is well below that level. I'd sell it to the Ring if I could, but I know they wouldn't buy it."

"You haven't tried yet."

He looked a bit perturbed. "I know the Ring a lot better than you do, Joe. It's a lot easier to get them to do what I want for you, instead of what you want from me."

If my hands were made of flesh and bone, they would have been palsied by then. "Tell me," I said.

"I can, like I said, get this feed analyzed by the best in the business. Plus I'll alert the Cybercops about the case and get them to check the area, check the backscans, all of it. I'll pocket the cost, because you've done us great work, Gates knows. We can also get you an alert monitor, if you really need help."

"This is something I need to get in my own hands," I told him.

"None of this conflicts with that. An alert monitor, which you'll wear, can summon help if you really need it. But you better need it like hell. Use it more than a time or two and they'll look on you like the Transmitter Who Called Woz. Understand?"

"Understood."

Kelly sighed, and wouldn't look me in the eye for a moment. Then he looked up. "Joe, I want to get you a helper."

"A what?"

"An assistant. Someone to help you out on this case. Let's face it, your judgment..."

"You're saddling me with a Junior Gee, Kelly? That's a laugh. I don't need some green-on-the-scene making static in my space. This is my thing. I'm doing it."

"And your judgment is clouded, Joe, because Alice means so much to you. I can see it."

I probably grated my teeth. "You ain't seen no-scannin' yet."

"That's what I'm afraid of. You want to go out there wired for hell, and you'll most likely get your heads parked. That won't get Alice back, and it won't help you, either."

"I know how to do my job, Kelly."

"Not this time you don't. Not where the woman you love is concerned."

Silence. A big, big silence.

"I never told you I loved her."

"You didn't have to, Joe. Anybody could see it for meters and miles. If I didn't care about you, I'd say, 'Do it,' and send you on your way. But it's not like that. Seeing you in a pile even Norton couldn't put together...that disturbs me."

The man had a sincere look on his face. I'd had my experience on the cyberstreets, sure. But I wondered how much experience he'd had, and I guessed it to be pretty vast. You don't get on the Ring without showing your gut circuits had gut circuits.

And brains? He probably outpointed me there, too. But I had enough rom and ram to get things done. For sure.

"Who you got in mind? I want to vet him before I accept."

"You'll have to take someone, Joe, and I think he's the best. The most promising out of our young pack. You'll be good for him, and he'll be good for you."

"Has he ever had either his heart or his chin broken?"

"Joe!" Kelly was emphatic now. "Shut up and let me bring him in."

I kept my jaws shut. Kelly withdrew something from a pocket he may have just manifested. "Send Denny thru, Mike. Yes, DNE3. On point, and no slower."

Holding the comlink at arm's length, Kelly waited, and he didn't have long to wait. Smoky matter started coming from the handset, and it coagulated within seconds. First the feet, in what looked like comfortable shoes. Then the legs, covered in what looked like brownish gold gabardine pants. We got to the chest, in a coat that matched the pants, a white shirt, and a red bow tie. His hands looked okay to me, but I wouldn't know until he had to hit somebody. Finally, the head filled in.

He modeled his hair, which was blonde, in a crew cut. It looked like he'd tried to put freckles in the appropriate places on his face, but he had one on his nose, said nose being kind of puggish. His eyes were green and gave a sense of eagerness. His lips were thin, and he was smiling.

"Joe," he said, thrusting out a hand. "I'm Denny. Pleased to meet you."

"The honor is all ours, son," I shook his mitt. No point in being mean, even to a kid who was still oiled behind the ears. We looked each other over and I have no idea if I looked impressive to him or just tired. "What's your pedigree?"

"Four lengths with the Ring Investigative Academy," he replied, still not letting go of my hand. "Top 15% of the class. Aided on the usual Cybercop cases and completed my intro case by myself. Illegal data-dumping."

I nodded. Gates knows, I'd been in his space before, but I came by way of Cybercops themselves, not the Academy. "Kid," I said after a time of silence, "has Kelly warned you what you're getting into?"

"He told me a bit about it, sir," said Denny, the smile off his face now. "Cybernapping your secretary. Nothing on the wall plate."

After a sigh, I said, "Kid, I've been working with Alice for a decent click of time here. Need I give you some examples which Kelly has probably given you already?" Kelly himself was standing there quietly, his arms folded.

"I got that she was very valuable to you, sir."

"Very valuable? Yeah. That's straight as a laser level, kid. I intend to find her, whatever state she's in, and bring the perp to—justice. With a little payback along the way. Capeesh?"

"Understood, sir."

"I don't think so, kid. You ever been in love?"

He took his time answering. "That's a personal question, sir."

"This is a datadragging personal case, kid. Talk to me."

Denny didn't look me in the eye. "There was somebody, once. It was a mid-season romance, I guess."

"Joe..." Kelly tried to interrupt.

I waved him off. "How was she?"

"She gave me everything," he said quietly. "And I doubt I'll ever see her again."

"Keep that feeling in mind, kid. It's way back on the point scale from mine, but it's as close to an understanding as we'll get today. Now. You do know that this show is on my ticket, correct?"

"Affirmed, sir."

"The guys we'll be interfacing with have paid their dues in stuff that's a very, very lot meaner than data-dumping, and they do it for a living. Do you know that you're putting your backplate in serious danger?"

He nodded. "We all have to face that somewhere."

"You'll be facing it a bunch. Can I rely on you to backstop me? Don't tell me yes if the answer is no."

"The answer is yes, sir. I'll burn my chips for you."

I shook my head. "I wish I'd had it like you when I was your age. But we all gotta learn sometime."

"Joe," said Kelly, softly enough.

I looked at him. "Finished with your interview?"

"We'll give him a try, Kelly." The kid seemed to stand up a little straighter.

"I'm leaving, Joe," Kelly concluded. "Gates help you both. Good luck."

With that, he put his hand on the wall plate and was sucked into it I couldn't even slo-mo it worth a damn. That kind of transport I couldn't afford.

"Let's do some analysis, kid," I said. "The day-cycle is still young."

It wasn't so young by the time we finished manipulating the holographic playback from the wall monitor. There were feeds in every room, and we attacked them from every angle. Denny had a good optic for detail but we both flunked out in trying to find any clues. After that, we checked the feeders that pointed to the area around the house. More motion there, but nothing that tripped our suspicions.

"A pro's pro," I told him, raking my hand thru my hair. "That's what I called him, and it's an understatement."

"Every unit slips up somehow, sir," Denny opined. "Just a matter of going thru the evidence enough times to show what doesn't grok."

"Listen. Don't throw out terms from Op Heinlein, and I'll try to stop calling you 'kid'. How's that sound?"

He beamed. "Affirmative, sir."

"And it's 'Joe', Den. That's the basis we gotta be on."

"Drive to drive, si—Joe. That's what we will be on."

"And in the case of where I learned about 'grok', I'm not illiterate. But I try." Big pause. "We're going to try the neighbors tomorrow. But if our guy transported in thru the wall plate, that's not gonna be a big help."

Sitting cross-legged on the floor, Denny situated himself a bit more comfortably. "Did Alice have any personal records around? I mean, like a blog or personal diary?"

"Den, I told her that if she ever blogged, I would tear the thing down to its lowest pixels and lower her salary." But something was nagging me, right in back of my memory board. "Do me something. Run it back to just before the black, and focus-freeze on the bedroom."

The kid 'faced with the wall plate in just the right way, and the pic of Alice in her blue nightgown within the bedroom turned up again. That image has since been burned into my RAM in a way that I'll never get it out, nor want to.

"Gimme some room, kid," I said, and Denny obliged. I put my fingers on the plate and manipulated the view carefully. First I got past that admirable figure of hers, then veered off to the side, right next to her bed. Enlarging the view, bringing up the brightness, zooming in on just what I sought.

I had a big pic of the stack of data discs beside Alice's bed.

"Count 'em, Denny. I already have. Tell me what you come up with."

He eyed the pile of discs. "Looks like 19, Joe. Is that what you got?"

"Kee-rect," I said, with the appropriate Op accent. "Now let's fast forward this bit."

We went back to black for a few minutes and then got the view of Alice's bedroom, alone. I froze it. "Now, Den, show me what the Academy taught you."

Denny brought up the view of the data disc pile anew. He took a serious glom at the picture, as did I, leaning over his shoulder.

"Eighteen. Eighteen of 'em, Joe."

"My count, too. And that, Denny, is what is technically known in the business as a clue."

⋧-⋦

After looking thru Alice's pile of data discs, we found not much more than bills, romance, comedy, drama, and maybe an instructional course or two. The courses were on writing and detective skills. I felt kind of sentimental about that, but kept it behind my firewall.

I let Denny say it first. "No diary. If she kept one."

"I think she did," I replied. "Or some other records that someone wanted."

"Or didn't want her to have," Denny offered.

"It all comes down to the same things," I stood up and stretched. "Did the plugger take her to get at her? Or to get at me? Or both?" Cracking my knuckles to get rid of some tension, I wondered why we never made a noise when we did that, and Ops did.

Denny leaned against the wall. "Joe, it would help if you filled me in some more on Alice's life. About all I know is that she was your secretary."

"Besides being beautiful and efficient and easy to get along with, mostly?"

"I kinda picked all that up, Joe."

"Well, she was the kind of fem who was looking for her way after matrixation," I began. "She graduated from BasicComp, but she really wasn't tracked with high credit earning skills. Not that she was dumb, just kinda unfocused. As to where she wanted to be." I hesitated. "There are lots of gals like that. And lots of gals that have a hard time balancing the ClickBooks."

"Dawn was like that," said Denny. "I hope she made out."

"Your sweetie?"

"Definite, Joe. Sorry to interrupt."

"No need to apologize. As to how I met her, she'd hooked up with a plug-guy who would pay the bills, which is what she needed at the time. He wasn't kind to her. I need not elaborate. A friend of hers asked me to intervene. I went over and intervened him all over the place. Once she was out of his hands, I asked if she could function as a secretary, and she said yes. That's where it started."

"I guess she must've been grateful."

"I guess she was." Short pause. "The guy was in no way a pro's pro."

"Kinda gathered that," Denny grinned. "Seemed too dumb to be, from what you said."

"However, that is an avenue to be followed," I took off my hat, shaping it, and putting it back on. "Denny, it's time you witnessed the fun side of investigation."

⇒-⇐

We took public transport to Cybercop Central. It moved somewhere between the speeds of light and sound but that was okay by me. I needed time to think and relax. The fury-fires threatened to burst out, but I couldn't afford that now.

The car we were riding in, painted pink to help stem such fires, had an ad on the opposite wall for the Rolling Numbers' greatest hits, including "Jumpin' Jack Crash" and "Get Outta My Space". There was a time I would've bought that, sight unseen. But I was older now. Denny was sitting beside me with his head a bit down.

"What's up, Den?" I asked, neutrally enough.

"I'm okay, Joe."

"Nervous?" He said nothing. I pressed on. "It's just Cop Central, kid. Can't be the first time you've been there."

"It isn't."

"So what's different this time?"

He clenched and unclenched his hands again. "Last time it was kinda theoretical. I had an Instructor to look over my work, every day. Had Cops to give my info to. I got to go on the raid, but I was in the VirtVan. The cops did the dirty work."

I stretched out my legs. "Getting schooled to going live. That's the way it is with every job, Denny. Look at me. Would you believe I was the greenest son of a W there ever was, when I started out?"

"No."

"That's because you're looking at me, version 8.5. I was strugglin' to be a One, back then. I worried about how I'd handle my first case, too. Out on the street."

"How'd it go?"

"Kinda like yours. Except I wasn't in the Virt Van." I chuckled. "I was still tough, but I hung one on the chin of the baddest matrixmangler in the gang. He returned the favor. It took half a cycle to wake me up. After I came to, they wanted to do something nice for me. They let me use the Snapcrackler on the guy to get a confession."

He smiled. "That's something."

"It was. But after that, I got wiser, got better at fighting, and, most importantly, picked my shots. Never forget that. Go to battle on your own terms, Denny. If you can't, find a way the hell out of there, fast."

Denny nodded. Still nervous, I judged, but managing.

"One more thing. Your first hit is your worst hit. After that, you're experienced. But don't seek it out, especially not on my time. Just wait, and let it come. Got that?"

"Got it. I've been thru self-defense training, Joe."

I gave him a good look. "Yeah. But not them-offense training. You still have an Instructor on this, kid. Me."

Denny eased up a lot more after that. But he still had some tension, which was natural and good. I'd have reprimanded him if he didn't.

The car got to Cop Central, dumped out everyone bound for it by withdrawing its existence from us, and continued on. Denny and I walked in side by side.

>-<

Si, a Cop whom I'd worked with before, saw us in at the front desk. An improbable smile cracked his fat features. "Joe! Where've ya been, chipster?"

I gave him back a smile. "Workin', Si. How's by you?"

"The same, only dumpier." There was no clue as to why Si had manifested himself as an obese Op in a Cop uniform. Maybe he'd seen images of such desk guys on YouTube vids and fashioned himself after them. If he'd had substance like in the Op world, and the chair beneath him, too, he would have reduced it to its component parts. As it was, we were in a pretty spacious anteroom with Si at a desk in the middle. There were about ten other males and females hanging around who were either waiting for help or waiting for more help. "Who's your friend?"

"This is Denny. He's my partner on this case. Give him your hand, Den." The kid was only too eager to shake the mitt of a professional. Si sized him up and gave a half-hearted shrug.

"How can I make life more easy, free-flowing, and sentimentally justified for you today?" he said.

"I'm looking for current whereabouts of somebody, provided he has any," I answered. Providing the guy's ID number was easy, and I did.

Si ran it through his databanks and frowned. "Thomas, aka Tomas Aggro. Several charges of plugmastering, one of them across lines. He's a bad 'un, but not bad-bad. Kind of medium level bad."

"Joe's dealt with him before," Denny put in.

"Den, please. Where's he at right now?"

Obligingly, Si rotated the screen to face us. It had two views of his latest manifested features, an address, an ID number, and a rap sheet. Both Denny and I scanned it and put it in our RAMs.

"That'll do, Si. Thanks. A lot."

Si got a bit more serious. "Just remember, Joe. When it's transmitted and done, you're not on the force anymore. Call us if it gets serious."

"I'll carve your number on my board," I replied. "Let's leave, Denny."

Outside, we went and waited for the next transport car. Denny asked, "Are we going for him tonight, Joe?"

"Why not? Anybody in there could have seen us looking at that screen. You ever been to the Deeps, Denny?"

"Well, no."

"I'll be glad to give you the grandest of grand tours."

The Deeps was a place I'd been to my share of times, but only when I had to. The last time was when I tackled that megalomaniac comp, Henry. It would become what Ops called the Deep Web, and if you wanted to commit any kind of cybercrime, that was the place to go.

We had a bit of advantage this time in that we knew where Tomas Aggro, as he now labeled himself, hung out. There were some crooks who could afford to slip away to other locations, if need be. Tommy couldn't do that. His business wouldn't allow it.

The two of us manifested at the closest port allowed. Luckily, nobody'd tried to assault us while we were firming up from feet to head. Denny and I were thrust into the outskirts of the Deeps, and I wasn't sure how he'd handle it.

He looked at me. "This guy is a pimp, isn't he?"

"Bluntly speaking, yes. Congrats on figuring it out. How'd you do it?"

Denny shook his head. "The way you said he treated your girl, and a couple of other things. I hate units like that."

My fists clenched by themselves. "I'm not overly fond of them myself. Let's interview that motherless plugger."

We walked on, more or less together. Artificial gravel ground beneath our feet. The sky was overcast, as it always seemed to be down there. The blinking lighted signs, there out of imitation of the Op world, were helpful for navigation. Cheap Expansion. New ID's. Plugging of every kind imaginable. Doorways to dens that, on the outside, euphemistically referred to psychoactive add-ons: "SO FAR OUT YOU'LL TOUCH THE CEILING OF THE WORLD", and so on.

And there were beggars. One of them, kneeling on the way beside us, manifested torn clothing so far out of fashion you couldn't track its era. He tugged on Denny's pants leg and Denny jumped back. The beggar made a sympathetic face. "Credits, sir? A few credits?"

"Don't," I warned him.

The guy flashed a multi-display of ugly stuff in his hand. "Pictures, sir? For only half a credit?"

Denny hadn't said anything. I told him, "Say no."

"No, thank you, sir," he hurried to be up with me.

He wheezed when he was up with me. "I've heard of it, but..."

"Yeah, 'but'. Welcome to the big city, Den. It gets more picturesque from here."

We proceeded. Cheap tarts flashed their plugins at us along the way. A dreamsmith offered us a great fix. Neither of us felt like saying anything. Our outfits branded us as outsiders, but we weren't slumming. Not this time.

"Why don't the Cops do something about this?" said Denny, practically in a private message.

"PICTURES, SIR? FOR ONLY HALF A CREDIT?"

"They do. But pretty soon after it's beat down, it comes up again. Some members of the Community, Denny, have needs the norm places can't fulfill. Opportunity meets need, and the place is back in business."

"One thing to know it in theory."

"This is where all theories are proven," I told him.

I think he swore at a very low level and I couldn't blame him. On the way, though, I could see him looking around, recording, piecing together the environment. Denny was trying to be a good detective, whether he wanted to be there or not.

"Pay attention to me, Denny."

"Sir."

"The place where we're going, I'm going to be smiling, like I've been to such places and I'm a regular. You're going to be a kid I'm showing the finer things of life, for the first time. Be nervous, but no more nervous than you are. Don't fake it. Capeesh?"

"Understood. I won't have to fake it."

"That's my chip. But keep control. I'll need you."

"Affirmative, sir."

I figured I could break him of the "sir" habit in time without having to slap it out of him. Maybe about the time I stopped calling him "kid". But I liked him.

After a few more sad streets we came upon the house of ill repute that was our goal. It was a double-story place with a roofed porch out front and, like the rest of the Deeps, had seen its better days. The windows on top were blacked out. In front, a couple of floozies manifested as tempting looks as they could with hardly enough clothes to suggest a mystery. They looked at us with that kind of look. I smiled back at them.

If Alice was in this place, I'd dismantle it to the ground with my bare hands.

"Evening, ladies," I greeted. "Anybody sportin'?"

A blonde sized us up. "Providin'."

Denny and I stopped within talking distance of her and her Asian-fashioned companion. He was looking at her a trifle too intently. She smiled and tossed her hair back.

"I have here a young friend of mine who has not yet tasted the pleasures life has to offer. Would this be the right place to educate him?"

"We can educate the hell out of him," the blonde smiled. "Let's talk price."

I lifted my hand. "Gettin' ahead of ourselves, we are. I want to make sure my pal gets the most transcendent experience this place can afford, to leave him with a memory that will last the rest of his natural term."

She chuckled. "Mister, looks like he's found the right person to experience him already."

Looking back, I saw Denny talking tentatively to the Asian girl. She moved closer to him and pressed her chest against his.

"Buddy!" I yelled. After a moment, he figured out I was talking to him.

"Yes, sir?" he said, like an unsure cadet.

"Get over here! We're talking business."

"Yes, sir," he said, somewhat mournfully. The Asian girl looked on him with scorn as he came over to me.

"Nice kid," I told the blonde. "But, ah, you know how they are at this stage of life."

"I ought to."

With my partner by my side, I laid on my shpiel. "As for price, we can negotiate. But in matters like this, you understand, my pard must have the best professional service possible. And that, ma'am, is why we must speak with the proprietor of this establishment and get his very own recommendation. Nothing less."

"You Cops?" she asked.

"Heavens, no. But everyone has needs. I have needs. Do we shop here, or do we look for another place?"

She thought it over. I guessed that she'd get beaten a lot more for not making a sale than taking a chance on Cops. "You want a plugging, too?"

"That would be the size of it, yes."

"We'll find out about size later. Gimme a minute."

She went into the doorway and closed the door behind her. While my attention was on it, I sensed someone beside me, turned, and saw the Asianette in front of me. She had done something with her breast manifestations, both enlarging them and covering them a little less. "How about you, sir? I give good plugin."

Denny was looking at me quizzically. I turned to her. "What's your name, girl?"

"NKE. You can call me Nikki."

"How'd you end up here?"

"Not important. I show you the secrets of the ancients, make you scream the name of your true love. How about that?"

I think I must have looked sad when she said that. At least, what I saw on Denny's face when I glanced at it seemed to reflect it. I closed my eyes, opened them, and put my hands on her shoulders.

"Young lady, you are a credit to your profession. Any other day, I would be happy to take you up on your offer. But, you understand, my mind must be clear when I negotiate for my friend. And I suspect you would leave it anything but clear for a good number of cycles. Understand?"

She seemed to smile, briefly. "You speak nice, mister, but nice words are empty. Once you are done with talk, you see me. I spoil you for all other women forever."

I had a notion she might do just that, excepting for one woman. "Thank you, Nikki. Thank you very much. Let us see what your boss has to say, and we'll take it from there."

She sniffed, turned her back on us—a back which she manipulated with great skill—and sat down in a chair in a corner of the porch away from both of us. Denny, coming closer, looked at me and put a hand on my shoulder. I appreciated it.

Shortly after that, the blonde came out, and above her head in the doorway I could see a plug-ugly (pun intended) who was at least a head taller than her and looked like he didn't have to enlarge himself to get that way. He gave us both a dull look but I knew he was scanning us hard. Denny was about to find out what he'd gotten himself into. So was I.

"You can come in," she said. "Follow us."

The ugly guy, who dressed in a black suit and boots, stepped aside to let the blonde, myself, and Denny thru in that order. He brought up the rear. Blondie, without saying much, led us thru a grey hallway with closed and open doors. Behind the closed doorways I could hear sensual buzzing of various kinds and verbal promises never meant to be kept or recorded. Through the open ones I beheld she-comps in various states of undress and beds that ranged from plain to elegant. They probably signified prices. Each of them gave Denny and me the eye and I tried not to give them much of one back. Denny checked each one, briefly. He'd learn.

We took a left turn at the end of the hall, went down a briefer one, and ended up before a locked, square-shaped steelite door. Nobody could get inside without considerable weaponry, or permission, I figured. It had the sheen of dull metal and a vocal input outside. Blondie activated it with a whisk of her hand. "They're here, boss," she said.

"Send 'em in," came a voice. "Rudy, too."

I still recognized that voice. But I didn't dare react to it as if I did. Denny was tense, but that didn't violate his character. Rudy, if that was his name, looked as concerned as an iceberg from the Op world.

Blondie placed her hand against the plate beside the input and things clunked behind the big door. It swung open, too quickly and without a sound effect. Behind it was a too-small space with another steelite door on the opposite side. I'd caught a vid called Space Odyssey or some such on the Tube and it reminded me of an airlock in that one.

"I'll let you all go," she said, almost apologetically.

"Uh uh," I grabbed her arm. "You're coming with us."

"Why?" She tried pulling away, but couldn't.

"Because I want you around. You can introduce us."

Rudy looked at me sharply. I gave him a smile back, not releasing Blondie. Denny's hands were beside his hips, looking like he was about to manifest something.

"I've got money to spend," I told Rudy. "I want her here for a second opinion."

The guy wasn't believing me, but probably figured he could handle anything that came up. Wasn't sure that wasn't true. The boss's voice came from another vocalizer. "Frisk 'em." .

Rudy gave us both the analytic eye, making us turn around and lift one foot at a time so he could check us for any minute irregularities. He didn't seem to find anything. I wasn't dumb enough to wear my Ring summoner, and Denny wasn't carrying. Blondie stood there breathing, probably weighing her chances on making a break.

"Clean," said Rudy.

The outside door swung shut and clicked closed. Then the inner door did that process in reverse. After it opened, I beheld another guard dressed in a white suit, as big as Rudy, but fashioned in the shape of a huge American Indian. If that was his fetish, so be it. The guy had his hands clasped on his knee; one leg crossed over the other, and was sitting in a transparent chair. They were the rage in furniture these days.

"Send 'em in," said the boss, from a vantage point just beyond us.

Myself, the blonde, Denny, and Rudy made a procession inward and the door screwed shut behind us. The Indian got up and stood beside the boss, who sat at a crystalline desk and looked about as cold as his desk's material. Said boss was an inch or two shorter than I, bald, black-mustached, and dressed in a light brown pullover shirt from what I could see. I knew what strength he had, but I knew what I had, too.

Denny, I thought, please, please, for both our sakes, don't screw this up.

The boss broke the silence. "I know you."

I could have given myself a disguise, true. But I estimated an honest confrontation would save time. I wasn't there to sample his girls. "I'm flattered, Tommy. Been some time, hasn't it?"

He paused, probably banking back his temper. "What in the pit are you doing here, you piece of data dump? And who's he?"

"He's a friend of mine. Thought I might show him your fine establishment, and let him pick what he wanted."

I'd let Blondie go and she was slinking up against the door. "Boss, can I go? Please?"

"No," said Tomas Aggro, not looking at her. "And you, lamefoot, call me 'Tomas'. If you want your heads in the same position."

"My, my," I smiled casually. "You don't even offer your guests a chair? How can you do business with such little consideration for clients, Tomas?"

He nodded at Rudy and the Indian. They materialized chairs for Denny and me, put them facing Aggro, and we sat down in them. Blondie remained standing and so did they.

"I will ask you again," Aggro said. "Why in the hell have you come here?"

I shifted position to make myself a little more comfortable. "Oh, Tomas, it's like this. You remember Alice? The girl who left your employ a number of cycles ago?"

He blinked red before he caught himself and returned to his normal skin-tone. "What about her? I haven't seen her. She's not here."

"You sure of that?" I leaned forward a bit. "Because somebody comp-napped her a night ago, Tomas. Although their skill set was probably a helluva lot advanced on yours, I figured you might have a line on the party that snatched her. How about it?"

"Told you, I don't know," he said, not much concealing the anger in his tone. "I've had no contact with that bytch since you took her. Nothing."

I'll give myself credit not for jumping across the desk at him. "Don't call her a bytch," I said, as quietly as I could without going inaudible.

The tension in the place went up +5 on a scale of 10. I would have rated it five out of five, but the scale had to be extended in this case. He snorted. "I call her a bytch because she is a bytch. She'd make a man with a plug like a whale wilt to a loose wire when he looked at her. I never once heard she made a John blow his gasket. When I plug her, I never come. I never..."

That was it. I was in automatic by then. Before either of his goons could touch me, I was over the desk, not touching it in the process. I grabbed his neck in one time and applied piston fists to his face. I wanted the back of his head to have a reverse impression of the front of it.

For an instant, I wondered about Denny. Mistake to the googleplex. Aggro kneed me hard, shoved me off him onto the pseudocarpet on my back, made some of his substance into a blade, and tried with all his strength to shove it in my face. I shot out my arms in a bit of extension, snagged his wrist with one hand, and poked him in the eyes with the other. He yelled in pain, but he wasn't done fighting.

Neither was I.

I slammed a kick to his midsection and knocked him against his crystalline desk, which cracked some and cracked him a bit, too. When I stood up to pound him, I was rewarded with spiking pain in both my shoulders. Craning my head around, literally, I saw Rudy behind me. He'd crafted his fingers into daggers, and they were impaling me on either side of my head.

Then, a miraculous miracle which, if it did not come from Gates, I'm sure he wouldn't mind taking the credit for. A sword chunked thru the right side of Rudy's head and out the left, with an arm on the end of it.

Denny's.

I registered the kid for one angstrom. He'd taken some damage, true, but he was probably better off than I was. The sword he'd manifested wouldn't crash the thug, but it would disrupt the hell out of him. No time to do a thankjob, though. I ripped out of Rudy's grasp, leaving some of my substance behind, and plowed back into Aggro.

Tommy-boy was growling, cursing, and generally proving himself an unworthy host. He fashioned his hands into knives and stabbed them at me. I rolled over the desk and under the knee space, which gave me a half-instant to think. The trouble is, most of us have gotten used to our Op-imitated forms. Only in situations of extreme danger did we think of shifting our substance into something potentially deadlier.

My partner had opened my mind.

I shoved up on the desk and sent Aggro, who was trying to get at me, sprawling. Then I activated a few impulses and did a little personal reconstruction.

When Tomas got to his feet and tried to charge, he found himself headed for a Joe porcupine.

I had studded my body all over with seven-inch spikes that nailed him in front when he ran into me and made him scream. Swiss-cheese holes were opening all over his chest. I made my spiky arms into a band and pulled him closer, till the spikes were coming out his back and he was hitting high notes that could have made him an opera star.

Then I shoved him away and let him plonk on his back beside the desk, leaking substance from a number of holes I was too busy to count. Aggro wailed, understandably. I deporcupined myself and wrought my right arm into another form. Tomas saw it.

"No, no, please! Please, Joe!"

To save words, which are precious, the blade of my battle-axe arm came down, several times, and severed his bottom half from his top half at the waist.

He screamed, and didn't stop till I hit him upside the head with the flat side of my blade. Aggro was still conscious. That was how I wanted him to be.

Finally, I had time to look around. Denny was standing there, cyberpanting in imitation of a winded Op. One of his arms seemed loose. Rudy was making spastic movements on the floor. The Indian was missing two legs and an arm, and something had been shoved in his mouth. He was sweating substance and trying to find a way to pull himself up. The blonde, looking fourteen shades paler, was shrunk against the door. She was probably the smartest of us.

"Denny, you done good."

He gave me a sincere gaze. "Thanks, Joe. Thanks."

Blondie said, "Mister, I…"

"Shut up for the moment," I said. Then I turned to Aggro. "Now, Tommy, what is to be done with you? I really, really do not appreciate your behavior."

"Please, Joe, don't crash me. You've got no idea how many credits I can give you. I've got plugees that make her look like basic quartz. I can…"

"Now, that wasn't a nice thing to say about the lady, was it?" I placed the flat of my blade up against his ear. "In this position, I could crash you pretty easily, Tommy. Wouldn't you agree?"

"Yes, Joe. Yes!"

"Alternatively, none of you are totally beyond repair. We could, or somebody could, get you to a disk doctor and put you all together nice and neat again. Well, maybe not as good as new, but who's complaining at this point?"

"Not me, Joe. What you want?"

I turned to Denny. "Keep your eye on Blondie, If she does something, act as if she's not a girl." To Tomas, I said, "You say you didn't have anything to do with Alice getting snatched. Is that so, Tommy?"

"It's true, Joe. I swear to Gates."

"I doubt you've seen the inside of a church since you were a chip. But I believe you. Now. Do you know anything about someone who might have taken Alice? Remember, I'm still not happy."

"No, honest, Joe. Never heard any rumors, no intel, no nothing."

"Uh huh. Who do you think might have had a reason to do this?"

He paused, awkward as hell with his chest looking like a golf course. "I...it...maybe..."

"Maybe who, Tommy?" I leaned it closer.

"Somebody..."

"Out with it. Now."

"The Chinks," he said. "The Octorad."

That one caught me out of the left lower quadrant. "The Octorad?"

"I don't know it for sure, Joe. But word is they've been snatchin' chippies all over the sectors. Guys over there like our kinda women, think they're exotic. So they've been grabbin' 'em, jobbing 'em, having 'em show their own gals how to manifest and act like them. It's good business over there."

"I'll just bet it is. I'll look that up. I wanna thank you for that, Tommy. But now, you need to do us one more thing."

"What's that?"

"I want you to let me lift you up, touch the wall plate, and open both of your doors. You pull any funny stuff; Denny here is ready to backstop me. So don't entertain such thoughts, Tommy. Get me?"

"Gotcha, Joe. Loud and clear."

I heaved his dripping, holey torso up, comphandled him over to the plate, and had him touch his gummy little hand to it. The door in front of us opened, and then the door to the house opened after it.

"Follow me," I told the other two, and went out first, followed by Blondie and Denny. I was carrying half of Tomas in my arms.

"Why are you taking me for?" he cried.

"Know how much I trust you?" I answered.

He didn't have anything to say to that. Once we were all outside the second door, I placed him down gently on his back just inside the airlock-style room.

"Oh, and Tommy?"

Tomas looked up, a bit nervously.

"What you said about Alice? That wasn't nice."

I turned my hand back into an axe and chopped his head off.

Blondie's mouth was open and she was trying to unleash a scream. Denny placed his hand over her mouth. I loved that kid.

"Joe," he said. "Why?"

"I owed him one. And I will call a Norton for him."

>-‹

Actually, I had to call a Norton for both of us. We'd both lost substance in that fight, and my GP, the original Norton, had us both lying on slabs beside each other in his clinic, with feeds dripping what we needed into us via our backs. Norton liked to affect green scrubs and was a bit overweight, with receding gray hair and glasses that didn't do anything but complete the image.

"Joe," he said, "if you want to get the dump beaten out of you, that's your business. But this guy? Really?"

"You oughtta see the other comp, Doc," Denny said with a smile.

"I can imagine," said Norton. "What are you into this time, Joe?"

"Bit of a kidnapping, Norton. Couldn't let this one go. Sorry."

"You're damn lucky they let you go," he huffed. "They left grooves in your back that I haven't seen this side of an industrial accident. Darn near ripped your back off. You think I can cure everything, Joe?"

"Well, so far you have, Norton. I'm most grateful. Heck, I recommend you to every crook whose face I've bashed."

He rolled his eyes and turned to Denny. "Sir, do you know that you've partnered with the most irresponsible, incorrigible, and prone to disaster guy in the entire Community, politicians and ministers included?"

"That's why it's fun," Denny said.

"Okay. About that fun, I reattached your arm, firmly, but give it a week before you really swing it. Those little holes in you ought to heal soon from the stuff I'm putting in you. Try to keep out of trouble, okay? And as for you, Joe, I've seen you worse. Maybe once. But you keep coming in here like this many more times, and nobody'll be seeing you again. Get me?"

"Loud and clear, Norton. I never get tired of the lilting sound of your voice."

"I'll send somebody in here when we're ready to unhook you both," Norton continued. "Joe, I would tell you to take it easy for a month. But I know you won't. So I'll tell you, watch your back. Literally."

"Got it."

"No, you don't. Or you'd do what I say. If you went up against somebody who really knew what he was doing—most likely, it'd be Crash City."

Neither one of us had anything to say to that.

"That's it," he said. "I'll send the bill to the Ring, as usual. Hope I see you both again, but not here."

We told him goodbye, and he left. Denny and I stared at the greenish walls of the clinic room for awhile, feeling the stuff go in.

"You really did call those guys a Norton, didn't you?"

"Hell yes, I did. Two working guys doing their jobs, and a crook too good to waste? It was my civic duty."

"You've got a heart, Joe. Ethics, too."

"Tell anyone else and you're off the case."

Denny stretched his arms and legs as much as he could. "I'm worried about you, Joe."

"I'm a little concerned about you, too, Den."

"Thanks, but I've gotta say this. Why'd we go to that plughouse? You said it yourself: this snatch was done by a pro's pro. I can't see this Aggro as anywhere near that."

"You're right, kid. But there was a chance he might know something about it, or that he might have hired a pro squared. He also gave us another thread to follow up. That's what he was: an outlying thread."

"There's something else, Joe. You lost it in there."

I gritted my molars and kept quiet.

"Joe, I'm sorry. But you could've gotten both of us Crashed."

"And i'm sorry about that, too, Denny, for your sake. You're right, I shoulda kept my hat on. Or I shouldn't'a got you involved. I was thinking, with about 50% of my mind, that I could talk to Aggro and keep it cool, get us both out of there alive. It could've happened that way."

"But it didn't, Joe."

"No. It didn't. Before you ask, Den, the other fifty percent of my thinker was rage. The kind you can't even touch with lead gloves. I've been firewalling this since Alice...since she got taken. Part of me was hoping he'd make a move. Just to let it out, to open the valve, at least partway. Hell, I wanted to lose control. For that, I'm sorry. But sorry doesn't cut it. I endangered you. I'm gonna have a long and nasty time living with myself for that."

Silence. I felt like I was in a confessional box at the Church of Gates.

"I want you off this case, Denny."

"No, Joe." He was as resolute as a data barrier.

"I can't handle it, Den. If you hadn't pulled those tricks back there, Gates help me, they would've Crashed you."

"They didn't. I was up in the top five of my self-defense class. The tactics I know, they probably didn't exist ten cycles ago. I can handle myself, Joe. Really."

Really.

"What're you getting out of this, Denny? The Ring stuck you in it, sure, but anybody else with a sane-chain on his ROM would probably have bailed by now. Talk to me, kid."

He made sure I was turned to look at him before he answered.

"I'm getting what they call a baptism of fire. Getting my hands deep down into it. I could've stayed in Analytics all my life and never seen the streets. But that isn't being much of a cop, Joe, or a detective. I need this."

I have no idea if I looked sympathetic or not. It didn't matter.

"There's more, Joe," Denny went on. "I can appreciate, a bit, what Alice means to you. If I can do anything to help you find her, I'm gonna. And you know why I'm gonna do it, Joe? Because I like you. That's all."

I kept my face shut and let the feed tubes at my back shhh pum away.

We didn't get out of Norton's office for the better part of a day. I was feeling better, but I made sure to tell Denny not to nudge the pain blocks, and told him what happened when Norton did, just to show me what it was like. Actually, Denny knew enough not to, but it was a war story. You always have permission to share war stories.

My office hadn't been occupied for three days. We transitted there and I went thru the messages on my wall plate, which weren't a lot. For the bills, I assured my callers they'd get paid. For the other customers, few as they were, I returned their calls, said I was on a big job, and referred them to other shamuses. Denny was probably recording all this for further research on How To Be a Detective, but he didn't let on.

After all that, I sat behind my desk with my feet on top of it. Denny was still by the wall plate. "Joe," he said.

"What?"

"What's our next move?"

"Well, my next move, Denny, is going to be into sleep cycle in a bit. I urge you to do so, too. I'll need all your circuits pulsing in the morning. Early morning."

"What happens then?"

"I contact the Ring. We see if Kelly can get us an in with the Chinese Cabal."

"Joe, I heard you had quite the time in the Deeps the other day," Kelly was on the screen of the plate's communicator.

"'The Deeps is the Deeps,'" I used a familiar quote. "Kelly, I need some leverage."

"What leverage?"

"Got a thread here that's headed Eastward. Can you connect me and Denny with the Chinese Cabal?"

"Why, Joe?"

"Think of eight limbs and it'll come to you."

Kelly's face sobered visibly. "You sure of this thing?"

Shaking my head, I told him, "Not sure of anything, other than Alice is gone and the guy I had a conversation with mentioned them. I have to follow it, Kelly."

"I can't authorize Denny on field work with this," Kelly said. "Those types are death viruses on wheels."

Denny stepped up. "I release you from all responsibility on this, sir. I'm going with Joe."

"That's really going to go over well with your matrix and your instructors. And with me. We wanted you to learn, not to get Crashed."

I piped up. "What if I leave Denny with the Cabal, and follow the lead, if any, alone?"

"I won't let you do it, Joe," Denny declared.

At that point, I turned, quite deliberately. "What did you say?"

"I said, I won't let you..."

"Like hell you won't! You do not refuse my orders, Denny. I'm in charge of both of us here. Am I clear on that?"

"Yes, sir," he hung his head.

"Let me hear it again."

"Yes, sir!" It was louder this time.

I moved closer in to him, but didn't touch him. "Stay with us, Kelly. Kid, if you intend to survive this thing, you do not refuse an order. You do not second-guess me. You do not look for logic–holes. And you do not disrespect me. Any of that, and you are out. Capeesh?"

"Yes, sir," he said, more softly.

"I am trying the best I can to make sure you don't get Crashed. You have no idea how dangerous it is where we're headed. Not so sure I do, myself. But at least I've got the experience to know what might be coming. You don't. I didn't ask for you to come here. This is about Alice, and it's my thing to follow thru on. You handled yourself damn well in that last job, Denny, but that ain't nothing compared to what the Octorad can do. Be glad I'm letting you go with me to the Cabal. Am I transparent on this, Denny?"

"Clear, sir." He stood a little straighter, and looked me in the eye.

"I'm only being this nice because I like you. Don't push it."

He nodded.

Kelly spoke. "If I can put in my own two bytes here, Denny, I'm going to see you get outfitted with a tracer on this one. Get the idea to follow Joe where he doesn't want you, and we'll know about it. Clear?"

"Totally clear, sir."

"Also, I'll make sure your graduation is revoked, and that you never get any closer to detective status than watching Joe on a crime report. Do you understand?"

"Perfectly, sir."

"One other thing, kid," I added. "When I was just starting out as a Cop, a guy named NLSN was my shepherd. He probably had more seniority, and had seen more street, than anybody else on the Force. He showed me all the cables, and I felt about him maybe the way you feel about me. If I'm lucky. And one day…"

I had to pause. Neither of the other two made a sound.

"One day, Nelson went out on a routine call for conflict resolution. Shoulda been easy. Shoulda been back before midpoint of the day. When we saw him next, he'd damn near been turned inside out. That's about how my heart felt, too, and it still does now, when I think of it.

"There's only so much luck out there, Denny. Don't press it too hard. Ever."

⋝−⋜

The transit down to the Cabal took longer than expected, but I'd never been there before, so there you are. Within a reasonable time, we materialized at a transit station. It was white and there were signs on the walls in UniComp language telling us where to go. Denny and I stepped away from the transporter so we wouldn't obstruct any newcomers. We could hear the voices of people on a level below us. I wasn't talking and neither was Denny.

Down the path the signs pointed out for us, there was an ID scanner. It bathed us in orangish light and recorded about everything identifiable about us. When it was done, two small screens hung in space before us. One had my picture on it and some writing below it. The other served the same for Denny. When they winked out, we knew to proceed.

The walkway took us down to the next level, which was packed with people, almost all manifested as Asians. Denny took the time to finally

"ONE DAY, NELSON WENT OUT ON A ROUTINE CALL..."

break his silence.

"How will they contact us, Joe?"

"They'll know," I said, still not looking at him. He hadn't earned it yet.

We barely made it off the walkway onto the debarking area when someone said, "Mr. Joe?"

Our attention was drawn to a red-suited Chinese gentleman in a red suit that looked even more formal than anything Kelly wore. "You are Mr. Joe, yes?"

"Got it in one," I said, smiling. "You'd be our contact, right?"

"I am, sir," he bowed slightly. "I am known as YNG, or Yung. We are honored to meet you."

Denny gave him a bow, too. I just stuck out my hand and he shook it. Yung said, "This is your apprentice?"

"You might say that, Mr. Yung. This is Denny. Denny, this is Mr. Yung."

"An honor, sir," Denny put in.

"A sublime pleasure to meet both of you. I will guide you to your transport."

First impressions shouldn't be that important. But I calculated I just might like this guy.

⋧⁻⋦

Yung took us to be Expanded first. It was a marvelous bar, with kimonoed waitresses, sharp-dressed barmen, exotic scans on the walls, and a yin / yang sign on the floor. The Chinese Ops might be communists, but the Chinese Cabal knew how to treat guests.

I was sitting between Denny and Yung, all of us plugged in by one hand apiece to the Expander plates before us. Since the incident the night of Alice's kidnapping, I took pains to watch my intake. Denny was trying manfully to hold on, but he hadn't the stomach for it yet. Yung pressed his plate lightly, let up, pressed it again at intervals.

"We have heard you performed great duties for the Ring," said Yung.

"I did a few jobs for 'em, thanks," I concurred. "What I've got in front of me might be the toughest job I've ever had."

He nodded, sagely. "The compnapping of your secretary."

"That's it."

"And how were you led this way?"

I took my hand off the plate to look at him. "Denny and I had dealings with a gentleman who knew her way back when. He didn't have the intel we needed, but he dropped a half credit on those jolly folks in your area who handle such stuff."

Yung grimaced. "Even our Ops know nothing of these matters."

"They wouldn't. I need to see your intel boys to see if I can set up a meeting with those guys."

Shifting on his seat, Yung took his hand from the plate and crossed his arms. "This is a matter of great danger, even for a professional such as yourself."

"Don't expect anything less."

"It would be advisable to give your data to our services and have them proceed," Yung went on.

"I intend to do just that. But I want the meeting, too. Your guys can backstop me if they want, or not. This is personal, capeesh? I want Alice back and I want to know who took her."

"It might be worth your life, Mr. Joe."

"It's always worth my life, Yung. Only this time, it's worth Alice's, too."

Yung seemed to understand. I heard a gurgling sound from my left and swiveled on my seat.

Denny didn't look good. "Joe, I respectfully request to withdraw to my room." A green warning shade had appeared about his gills. I sighed.

Then I snapped my fingers. "Waiter!" When one came up, towel over his arm, I said, "My friend here has had too much. He needs help getting back to his room." I gave him the coordinates.

"But of course, sir," the waiter bowed and hustled Denny off the stool and towards the transport plate in the wall.

Denny almost got there before he threw up on the floor.

The next day we were at whatever the Cabal called their intel department. Could have been Dragon Central, for all I knew, but I wouldn't say that in their faces.

The boss of the outfit, or at least the one who was talking to us, was CNG, or Chang. He had slicked-back hair and wore a golden decorated robe with big sleeves that hung down below his arms. When he was in the office, I guess he could dress the way he wanted. There were a couple of silent flunkies near the walls, and as far as I could tell, their eyes never left us.

Denny was also silent, but I hadn't ribbed him about his problem. Chinese Expanding can be hard stuff.

"So, Mr. Joe, you want us to set up a meeting between yourself and the Octorad?" Chang asked evenly.

"That's it, sir," I answered.

"What do you expect to get out of it?"

"What I keep telling everyone, so far. My secretary's been compnapped. A hood in my sector clued me that the Octos are behind a lot of snatchings in our area, for the plug trade."

He clenched his hands in front of him. "This is no great secret. But if your secretary has been taken by the Octorad, the wisest course would be to value her memory, and move onward."

"Guess I'm just not that wise, Mr. Chang. Alice means a lot to me. A Googleplex wouldn't cover it. Either I get her back, or I Crash trying. I trust my intentions are clear."

"Very clear, Mr. Joe," Chang nodded. "But organized crime is far deadlier than the street variety. The Octorad is macrolevels beyond the orgs in your sector. You cannot get past them with just your fists."

I sighed. "I can upchat with the best of them, if I need to. I don't anticipate a brawl."

"You might do well to anticipate a quick and very efficient assassination."

"I'll put that in my top file. But there's only so much talking we can do. I take it, Mr. Chang, that you have the power to broker a meeting with me and the Octos?"

He paused. "We would not have the power to interfere."

I smiled. "Here's what I want to do."

$$\succ\text{-}\prec$$

Getting a seat at the table of the Cabal's underworld wasn't quite as simple as transiting to the Deeps. The Octorad was at least as sophisticated as Chang's org, and I couldn't testify as to who could wield more power in a fight.

I had left Denny in the hands of Dragon Central and went back to my room alone. After a sleep cycle, I was roused from bed by the wall monitor, letting me know I had a message. Putting my fingertips to it, I saw static on the video and heard a masked voice.

"In the lobby," it said, and that was it.

I snatched myself some nourishment from the room bar, manifested some clothes, and transited down to the lobby. Almost before I could step off the transit circle, there was someone beside me. He was on the small side, very formal, and very intense. He had a smile on his face and the usual black three-piece suit on his frame.

"Mr. Joe?" he said.

"When last seen," I quipped. "And you are?"

"I am Koto. We shall take you to your destination."

"We?"

I couldn't tell where the next party came from, if he'd just transited in behind me or if he had hidden somewhere like a ninjabot. But Koto's companion was a gigagoon to the third power. He was taller than me by two heads, and the head he wore had a grim expression on it. He had so much body to cover with the black suit he manifested that I was sure it must be a power drain to maintain it.

Almost gently, he took the Ring tracker off the back of my wrist. I was not happy about that. But given the state of things, I didn't have much I could do about it.

"Okay. Take me."

⋝–⋜

And they took me. They took me through a direct transition station.

Thanks to the dematerialization and materialization, I had no idea of where we went. Nobody had to put a Silence Bag over my head. But when my feet touched flooring again, I was still between the goon and Koto. It was in an office somewhat more elegant than Chang's, hung with more scans d'arte and boasting more 3D and 4D sculptures, with a bigger, more ornate desk.

The personage who sat behind that desk was more quiet, more conservatively dressed, and more slowly paced than Chang. He had a full head of hair which was white as snow, and his eyes remained half-lidded. Both of his elbows were on the desk, and he was twining and untwining his fingers unconsciously, or so it seemed to me.

There were gunnies in all four corners of the room and only one narrow doorway.

"Mr. Joe," he greeted me. "I am Ling."

"Thanks for seeing me," I responded. A quick reference of my data banks informed me that Ling, in Chinese, meant Zero. A reassuring thought.

"Koto, Huihuai, go to the next room," said Ling.

As they exited, I said, "Don't mess with the tracker. It'll activate."

"And if it does, my guest, you will deactivate in seconds." Ling didn't have to emphasize his words.

"Wouldn't expect anything else. May I sit down?"

"Of course." Ling gestured and someone dragged up a comfortable chair, which he placed in front of and to the left of the desk. "I know something of why you requested this audience."

"My secretary got compnapped," I confirmed. "I have no idea whether or not your org had anything to do with it, but I was given the impression by a pimp I dealt with. If you can help me get her back, I'd be grateful."

The man was silent for a good moment. "This man implicated us?"

"Not directly. He said it might be, and I quote hjm, 'the Chinks', unquote. There are reports that females from my sector have been kidnapped and taken to the Cabal for plug slavery."

"And he was a procurer," said Ling.

"Exactly."

Another pause. Then Ling said, "Do you have data on your secretary?"

"I do." I produced a disc from my pocket. Ling took it, put it in his hand, and let a holoimage of Alice materialize before us. She was wearing a red blouse and a very short pleated white skirt.

"A most attractive woman."

"I've found her so, yes."

He looked at the stats and identifiers that accumulated under her image. "A few moments, please," he said, and made a gesture with the hand that wasn't holding the disk.

A very quick series of deliberately blurred images passed thru Alice's hologram and statistics did the same thru her identifiers. I wonder how many women with broken lives would fit those profiles, but, sadly, they were not my objective.

Within instants, the process was done. "She does not stat-match anyone in our records," said Ling.

"And all of your...women...are recorded in that 'base?"

"If we find a hunter holding out on us, he takes her place. There have been no more than three such incidents in my lifetime."

I sat a bit easier in my chair. Only a bit. "So you would say that this is an accurate indication that she is not in your employ?"

"I would."

"Thank you," I extended my hand. "I would like my disc back, please."

He didn't give it back. Within an instant, the four gunnies weapons were at my throat.

"I have provided a service, Mr. Joe. I expect a payment."

Without hesitation, I hollered, "DENNY!"

In the next room, the Ring tracer started a banshee howl.

For the first time, Ling's eyes widened.

"Unless I countersign, Ring ops will transit down here at a speed you won't believe. They'll have weapons that'll clean out this rat's nest, you included. Kill me, and they'll do it faster. Break that tracer, and there'll be no way I can countersign. Best guess, you've got ten seconds."

Ling didn't ask if I was bluffing. He made a sign, and the gunnies withdrew. I went in the other room, saw Koto freezing up against a wall with an arm in front of his face, and the goon holding the tracer in his palm and stabbing at its circular face with one big finger, to no avail. It was still howling to rouse the ghosts.

"Give me that," I said, and snatched it out of his hand. I put it on my wrist and said, "Hold it." The howling stopped. Then I sauntered back into Ling's office.

The director was standing behind his desk now, silent, but with a look of fury. The gunnies looked nervous. I put my fists on his desktop and looked him in the eyes.

"The Ring knows where I am now, and it knows where you are. I doubt they know who you are, and if you let me go, I won't tell them. Also, I made 'em agree not to hit you if I'm released. But if I don't report back very quickly, all bets are off."

"Bluffing, you are."

"Do I really have to say, 'Try me'?"

His guards could have Swiss cheesed me in instants, and I had no doubt they'd Crash me doing it. But Ling gave no signals, either verbally or any other way.

"Very well, Mr. Joe, be seated." I obeyed. "But the fact remains, I have given you valuable information."

"In a negative way, yes. I was hoping for another lead on Alice, though."

"What if I told you that I could help you in your quest?"

I didn't say a thing.

"The reach of the Eight Arms is beyond your understanding," Ling went on. He was seated behind his desk, now, and his eyes, though no longer half-lidded, were bereft of fury. "I may pass along the stats and image of your woman to them, with strict instructions to notify you if she is seen."

"And in return, I have the Ring erase all data on the whereabouts of this place?"

Very slightly, he smiled. "That would be a satisfying bargain by my standards. I dislike the cost and effort of moving."

"Deal." We shook on it. "Now, I want to go home."

"Of course." Ling snapped his fingers and Koto and the gigagoon came inside. "Escort Mr. Joe back to his hotel room, without damage, and quickly."

"Just Koto. No offense to your other guy, but he and I have a better relationship."

"As you say. But Koto must be returned to us unharmed."

"Of course." Hearing that, Koto looked relieved and Big Huey, whatever his real name was, seemed disappointed.

As Koto started off with me, Ling said, "One more thing. As a businessman, I applaud you, Mr. Joe. I know of your reputation, and you have more than lived up to it."

"Thanks for the hospitality."

"And one final thing," he looked serious. "When you find this man and kill him—let me know."

⇒-⇐

Koto and I returned to our point of departure, right back at the trans station. He smiled in relief. "This has been a great privilege, Mr. Joe. But we will never see each other again."

I made sure the tracker was firmly on my wrist. "They can't trace you thru this station?"

He shook his head. "We have passed thru an immeasurable amount of way-stations. Not even my org could track us without permission."

"Permission from your boss?"

"Exactly." The smile never left his face.

"You've been a great help, Koto. Thanks."

"A pleasure," he reentered the station and zipped himself away. I hadn't shaken hands with him. That was deliberate.

Hoofing it back to the hotel, watching the bikini bunnies playing in the virtual pool outside, I got into the lobby of the redstoned building and saw a familiar person walking up to me.

"Mr. Joe," he extended his hand. "You have done the unbelievable. May I welcome you back?"

"Sure, absolutely, Yung." I hid my left hand behind me, the one with the tracker on it, and extended my right for a shake. Yung raised one eyebrow, but he shook my hand.

"Will you allow us to examine the tracker? Or can we be second after the Ring does so?"

"Neither. When I make a bargain, I keep it. The deal was that we wouldn't reveal his base of operations, and I'd get intel. Which I did."

"Excellent, Mr. Joe. But our concern in this matter is the access you got to the org's location, or at least your contact's office. Now…"

Not unlike Ling, he nodded his head and some plainclothesmen started getting up from lobby seats.

I took the tracker off my wrist, threw it on the floor, and stomped the hell out of it. Spread the very small fragments all over the carpet, and picked up a bit of the resulting dust and swallowed it.

Yung's men were surrounding us both. He was looking very displeased.

Automatically, a cadre of Ring soldiers materialized around us all. They had the kind of weaponry even I couldn't ID, and the tourists at other points of the room were gaping, pointing, and whispering. The soldiers had been automatically summoned when I busted the tracker. I raised my hand and said, "It's okay, boys. I did this."

The Ring men shouldered their weapons. I had a big datadump-eating grin as I faced Yung.

"I'd like to see Denny, please," I said.

ⱬ–ⱬ

When the concierge got me back to my room, I opened the door and Denny practically jumped at me. "Joe!" he enthused. "You're back!" He threw his arms around me and hugged me.

Smiling, I hugged him back and disengaged his arms. "Steady, Den, you'll give them all ideas. How are you?"

"Swell, Joe. It was great hearing you call my name and listening in when you jawed that guy. I'll never be half the comp you are, believe me."

"You better forget anything you heard, brother. It's dangerous." I went past him into our room and saw another sight for sore oculars.

"Evening, Joe," said Kelly, sitting on Denny's bed. "Must say, I'm relieved you came back with all your pixels."

"Makes two of us, Kelly," I shook his hand. Denny was beside me after shutting the door. "What's the scoop?"

"The Cabal is not happy with us," Kelly said. "They were counting on that information to mount operations against the Octorad. I heard from Chang about that."

"Did you tell him if I turned that tracker over I'd probably be Crashed before the next cycle?"

"Something like that," Kelly grinned.

"Joe could've fought 'em off," said Denny, earnestly.

"At ease, son," said Kelly. "We've got the data held, Joe, but nobody's looked at it yet."

"Wipe it," I said. "I want to stay alive at least till after this is done."

Kelly sighed as Denny sat on my bed. "This info is gold to us, Joe."

"Alice is platinum to me."

He activated a tracker of his own, gave some coded orders, and then looked up. "It's done, Joe."

"Thanks. I appreciate that. Now I guess it's back to our sector."

Denny said, "It might not be that easy, Joe."

I turned to him. "Whaddya mean?"

"The Cabal has turned off our access to transit outside their sector. I'll bet they won't let us out until we give them the info they want. We can't give 'em anything now."

"Who needs them?" Kelly chuckled. "You've got me."

He twisted the lens on his tracker and the three of us were gone.

⋗⁻⋖

I don't know if Denny had ever been up to the Ring level before, but he didn't act like it. The first glimpse he got of the place was enough to make him pie-eyed.

"You can show him around if you want, Joe, but don't go too far," Kelly suggested. "Something I have to do."

"Sure," I gave Denny as much of a tour as I thought would be good for him. He touched some exhibits and said, "This is beautiful", more than once. Fine by me, even if some of them were representations of juicy Crashings.

A short while later, Kelly got us both back down thru the wall plate in my office and we materialized with great efficiency.

Once we gathered ourselves up again, Kelly leaned against the wall and spoke to me. "The Cabal aren't the only one disappointed here, today, Joe."

"Who else has my charming persona not worked for?" I poker-panned.

"Cut the laugh juice," he said, irritably. "The Ring isn't happy, either. They expended agents on a high-level guarding duty, they found the coordinates of one of the biggest crime syndicates in the Community, and now they've had to dump the data."

"Tell them I sincerely appreciate that. But the Octorad knows me now, and they know Denny, and if they think I've finked on them, both of us are gonna get Crashed at least a dozen times apiece." The kid looked at me, knowingly, but kept silent.

"I mentioned that to them," said Kelly. "They took it into account, but they're still not happy. There's gigas of plug slavery cases, Crashings, credit launderings, you name it, we could have cleared up with that data. Measuring that up against the fate of one guy, or even two, it was hard to balance the weights."

I pulled up a chair and sat backwards in it. Kelly had to finish his shpiel.

"They wanted to put you in Protection," he continued. "I told them that was only temp, where the Octorad was concerned. That part was understood. They argued that we could hit the 'Rad so hard, they might not be able to take revenge on you. You can imagine what I told them. We stalemated."

Denny looked like he was about to burst forth with paragraphs, pages, the complete scan of a Russian novel. But he tamped it down, and waited.

"What'd they say, Kelly?"

Long pause.

"They don't want to expend that many resources on this case anymore, Joe. They don't want me tied up so much with it."

"But Joe has saved the backplate of the whole Community before!" Denny said, jumping up and getting in Kelly's face.

"Kid," I warned him.

"They ought to know that, Mr. Kelly," Denny wouldn't stop. "The Community owes him everything. The Ring owes him everything. And this, Mr. Kelly, is important to Joe. His, well, his potential cybermate has been stolen. He loves her, and he's, well, he's hurting. I can see that, Mr. Kelly. Can't you see that too?"

The three seconds of pause after that was the longest time of my life.

"The Ring decides who they owe, and who owes them, Denny," Kelly reminded the kid as gently as I've ever heard him.

Denny wilted a little, looking sad.

"And it's just because Joe has been a miracle worker, more than once, that we're giving him as much as we are now. I know what love is, son. Back at my unit, there's a woman that's been with me for many cycles. I pray to Gates you get one half as good as her for yourself. Also, I know about hero worship, Denny. I know that Joe's your hero."

He almost collapsed at that. I took him by the arm.

"I like this kid, Joe. It's your decision as to whether he stays or goes."

I took just as long answering back.

"Kelly—he stays."

Denny seemed like he was almost in tears.

"Keep filing your reports, Joe, and keep going," Kelly said. 'I'll try—repeat, try—to get you another tracker. But I'd advise you to make sure that whatever you get into from here on in, you can handle it yourselves."

Then he touched the plate. "And Joe? In case you didn't know it, you're my hero, too."

And he was gone.

I had Denny weeping on my shoulder after that. I didn't discourage him a bit.

After we both had a sleep cycle, we got up and I had him as my second pair of scanops. We'd had Alice's wall monitor scans imported into my plate, and we went back at least a month on the thing. What little we could make out when her image recorded some data on the disk in her hand didn't amount to much.

"I'm sorry for the way I acted on this one, Joe," Denny was still scanalyzing the image of Alice doing what she did best.

"Sorry for what?" I didn't take my eyes off the screen either.

"You know. Telling you I was going in with you."

"You've apologized for that."

"Then getting drunk, and puking, and talking to Mr. Kelly like that. And crying, for Gates's sake. I wouldn't blame you, Joe, if you'd dropped me."

"Well, I might have," I sent the hologram a little further forward.

He didn't say a thing, as usual in these circumstances, so I plowed on. "Den, your mistake so far has mostly been trying to act a thousand cycles older and two thousand more experienced. You act like you're trying to be me. That won't work, Denny. Not yet."

"When do you think?"

"Irrelevant. You'll understand when you're there, if you get there. You keep working as hard as you have, you keep being as smart as you are—"

"Smart, Joe? You think I'm smart?"

"Oh, yes. Not enough sense yet, but smart you got. Regarding the puke, there's not a guy around who hasn't made that kind of performance. More than once. Now you know a little better how to handle your Expansion."

"I won't do it anymore."

"That'd be just as bad as overdoing it. Just take it easier next time. You'll learn. Trust me on that."

"Okay, Joe, I will."

"About you standing up for me in front of Kelly, you're right. I should've whacked you for it. But I started seeing the effect you were having on him. Worked in our favor. He understands you a bit more. He likes you, kid."

Denny snorted in friendly fashion. "I don't even mind you calling me 'kid' anymore."

"I'll try to leave it out unless I can't think of anything else to call you. Finally, in the case of you watering my shoulder last night, if you tell me you're sorry about that, I'll belt you. Understand?"

"Understood, Joe."

"That's normal comp emotion. If you think I haven't done that before, or any Cop I know hasn't. I could give you a good long education on that matter. But I won't. Hell, before this is over, I might be crying on your shoulder."

He looked at me sincerely. "Don't hug me, and keep your eye on the holo."

But we didn't find a hell of a lot more.

Den and I sat down at a table, near each other. "Drawing any conclusions?" I asked him.

"Well, first off, he didn't leave any traces on that pile of disks. You've checked on that and I understand the Ring did, too."

"Definitely," I leaned back and putting my hands behind my head. "What else?"

Denny scratched his chest, absently, the way he'd seen Ops do. "The length of that blackout on the tape is interesting. How long did it take him to overpower Alice? Did she fight back? From what you told me, she would have."

I nodded.

"If she did, he would've had to spend a lot of time putting the scene back as it was before he came in. That would account for a whole bunch of blackout there. We know he went back and wiped the time just before he arrived, however long that was."

It was a great idea to let the kid speculate, so I did.

"Supposing he had enough power to immobilize her and send her through the transit without much interference," Denny said. "Even so, why did he take time to go through those disks, find out which one was her diary, take it, set up everything as it was, and wipe it clean? How'd he know what was on it?"

"He might not have known it," I put in. "But he could have suspected.'

Denny eyed me. "That wasn't something I considered, Joe."

"Keep going."

"Even if he did pad out the blackout time on the wall plate, the perp did spend a whole lot of time in Alice's place," Denny extrapolated. "Say he just wanted to snatch her, and came prepared. Even if she fought back, it shouldn't have taken as long as the blackout."

"My sentiments exactly."

"And so far, he hasn't told us anything," Denny concluded. "That probably means he had something personal against Alice. Do you think Aggro could have hired him, Joe? Like you said, a pro's pro?"

"I don't think Aggro was the least bit interested in snatching Alice," I sat up and clasping my hands in my lap. "If he had, he'd know he'd have to face me. Even given those two hunks of hard drive he had with him, you know how that'd turn out."

"I know how it did, Joe."

"The Octorad was probably no more than a good guess. They were compnapping women, Aggro knew about it, and he implicated them to save his circuits. I understand they still haven't finished putting him back together, let alone his thugs. So we were off on a wild impulse chase. Not that it didn't help."

"Yeah," Denny recalled. "We found out they don't have her, and they offered help."

"So," I stood up and shoved the chair away. "We have three strong possibilities. The perp took Alice to hurt her, or to hurt me, or to hurt us both."

"But wouldn't he want you to know who he was? To tighten up the base screws?"

I took my time about answering. "You're damn right he would, Denny."

"So why hasn't he made any kind of contact, or left any kind of clues?"

Probably the time I took was what's known as a dramatic pause, but I never took drama in matrixulation. It was just me putting off trying to tell him.

"Because he thinks I can find him."

꒰⊱⊰꒱

"AND SO FAR, HE HASN'T TOLD US ANYTHING."

I set my sleep cycle for a double run. It'd been a long week or so, and I needed it. Time to recover, time to dream maybe of a solution, time to dream maybe of Alice. In dreams, I didn't have to be efficient. In dreams, I could love her, pretend she was here, and not keep all my feelings in a Mobius loop. In dreams, I'd be as free as I ever could be.

So I told Denny to keep watch over things while I was asleep and he wasn't. That'd give us one cycle of coverage. It should be enough, I wagered.

And I slept.

I'm not sure about Op dreams, but comps can't record those sleep-plays any better than humans can. If we're lucky, and the dream is intense enough, we can recall some parts of it, bits and pieces here and there. Some say dreams can give you clues about your life. But that wasn't what I was hoping for. Me, I just wanted relief.

Somewhere along the way, Alice entered into my dreams.

It wasn't like she gave herself a big intro or not. As I recall, we were at a dance, and without warning, the fem I waltzed with turned into Alice. She was wearing a spectacular ball gown and I swore, if I got her back, I'd buy her one just like it.

Her touch, the temp of her body aura, the sound of her voice, all of that put me into a sense of immense security. I was not afraid to let her know I loved her, here. She was talking as we danced, but I don't recall much of what she said.

That is, until she said, "When will you come get me?"

She was still warmly smiling. I managed to say, "I've been trying."

"When are you coming to get me?" she murmured. We were still dancing, and she rested her head on my shoulder as she said it.

"Look, honeychip, I've been trying. Really, really trying. Can you tell me where you are?"

Alice pushed away from me, gently, then. She still had that smile, one that could save half the Community on their power bills.

"When?"

That was all she could say before she did a fadeout.

I think I was dumbstruck at that point, and I had a right to be. Did I go after her? Did I search every nook and cranny of the Dreamworld? Don't know. Don't know.

There was, as best I recall, some other stuff. A maniacal laugh someone was trying in vain to control with a graphic equalizer. A gigantic atom containing all the stuff in the universe fizzling out and dying, instead of Big Banging. A huge old chronometer in the sky, ticking away but showing no time.

Nothing, really, that'd give me an edge when I woke up.

The most intense dreams come just before waking, or so I hear. If so, what I saw next was Denny's face. I didn't want to wake up to that, so I went back to sleep.

≥-≤

Eventually I did get up, sluggishly remodeled my appearance, sent my PJ's to the closet and selected a casual outfit to wrap itself around my body. Plus a hat. I never went anywhere without a hat.

Before I went into the kitchen for my usual jolt, I heard Denny in the front room. "Good mid-cycle, Joe."

"Yeah, you too," I charged myself with light nourishment for the brain. "Anything new?"

"I've been working on it," Denny sat cross-legged in his pajamas in front of the wall plate. "A little."

For him, a little might be the equivalent of a degree dissertation. "So what? Any amazing breakthroughs?"

"Just some thoughts, Joe." Denny brought up something on the plate monitor. It appeared to be criss-crossing and non-crossing lines, in a 3D hologram. He rotated it a bit to show all sides, top and bottom as well. "This, as near as we can figure it, is the record of all transits in this subsector the moment the blackout started. As you might guess, nothing shows an approach to Alice's house."

"That's what we know so far," I conceded. "But I'll lay credits you didn't call me in here with a happy face to tell me you've got nothing."

"Not quite. I've run it up a bit—" He gestured to the hologram and it changed configuration. "—And back as well." It went back to the previous image, and ran a bit in reverse. "Even given that our guy went and wiped out the intel to before he got there, we still have no tracker on him."

I sat in a chair facing him. "And you're just waiting to throw a 'but' in there."

He grinned. "But. It took a lot of doing, but I got a halfway decent plotting point on where the transit could have originated."

I pushed myself to a standing position. "Where?"

"Took a helluva lot of plotting, positioning, and calibration, plus guessing, Joe. I begged for some help from the Cops and Transit Control and dropped your name. Mainly, we weren't checking for where a transition was. We looked for where one should be, but wasn't."

"Den, I didn't ask you 'how'. I asked you 'where'."

His fingertip picked out a point in the midst of the 'gram. I knew enough about reading maps to get a handle on where he was pointing.

"Maybe—there."

My hands were clenched unconsciously. "Get dressed, Denny. We're on our way."

"We?"

"You betcha, kid."

>-<

The geography of the Community's world does not, from what I've seen of maps, conform much if at all to that of Earth, the Ops' world. But what they would call the "American Sector" was independent of the "Chinese Sector" and the "Australian sector' and so on, depending where the Ops were located. You still needed some ID to travel between such places, and why not?

The place we were headed for was in the European sector, apparently due to the continental Ops. Specifically, it was in the Sicilian section. That made me think of Guillermo, aka the Sicilian, and the case of the Black Virus. But he'd been separated into his component parts and he was no threat. None of the extant pieces had any memory of what he'd been or what he'd done.

The transit station where Denny and I ended up wasn't as opulent as the Chinese Cabal. It was more down to earth, or down to lower-level Community standards, than my last stop. The folks down there manifested clothes less on the businessman side and more working-class. Overalls, T-shirts, pants, comfortable shoes, and several old rich folks who had made themselves look fat and well-dressed, usually with a diamond-style ring on their pinky.

Denny stepped off the transit space and looked around. "Never thought I'd get to travel as much as I have on this case."

I stepped off and joined him. "Most cases aren't like this. They're usually local. Let's go see our brethren."

A mustached attendant at the greeting desk gave us coordinates for the Hall of Justice in that subsector. I thanked him and tipped him a credit. Denny smiled at him, but seconds later looked neutral again.

"This may be a stupid question, Joe, but when do you think you'll get back your tracker?"

"Don't know, Denny. Unless Kelly is mighty convincing, or even wants to be, I may not get it back."

"After all you've done for them?"

"We've gone over this before. If it was Ring business, I'd get carte blanche. But this is more in the nature of, well, a vendetta. Any help on this is sheer froth on the Expansion dose."

"I capeesh," he sighed.

"You don't have to come with me if you don't want," I reminded him.

"I'm seeing this thru, Joe. Street experience, remember? And friendship."

"Okay," I guided us to the nearest public transit service.

⇒-⇐

The Cop Chief, looking somewhat slimmer than other persons of authority I'd seen there, had a crisp grey uniform, a decent thatch of black hair, a modest mustache, and eyes that showed both friendship and no-nonsense. He pumped both our hands.

"Mr. Joe, we still remember your work in the Guierrmo case. It is a pleasure to meet you."

"Thanks, Chief, and double for me. This is my partner, Denny, and he'll show you what we're looking for."

Denny, obligingly, stepped up and brought up the hologram between his hands. "Joe and I have been looking into an abduction case. His secretary is the one who was abducted."

The Chief, leaning with his buttocks against his desk front, nodded grimly.

"The perp was a superpro," I said. "Wiped all traces from the event. But Denny was able to dig up some stuff here that led us thisaways."

"So you think your man is from our sector?" the Chief said.

"Don't know that, or if it was just a bystation he used in transit. But it's the best lead we've had so far."

"This is where we were able to make the most logical projection," Denny pointed out a red pinpoint on the holomap.

The Chief squinted at it. "Ai, this is not so good. The indication is, well, the Palude. What you would call the Swamp."

"We call ours the Deeps," I said, "but I get the picture. Pretty much Crime Central, right?"

"Our sector council would not refer to it as that. But yes, that is a fairly accurate description."

"We'd appreciate…" Denny started.

I cut him off. "Yes, we would appreciate any info and any help you could give us. Including manpower, if we can get it. I want to find the scum who did this and I want Alice back. If she can be brought back…"

Long pause. "Uncrashed," I added.

"I understand, Mr. Joe," the Chief nodded. "But remember, we cannot authorize a vendetta. If you find the perpetrator, if you apprehend him, you must turn him over to us."

"Granted. But I won't rule out having a little fun with him first."

Again, the Chief smiled. "I would not expect anything less."

The next day, the two of us went back to the Cop shop and were assigned a pair of guards or aides or guys on special duty. Whatever you wanted to call them. They were young, one was named Matteo, and the other was Lorenzo. They seemed like stand-up guys, but they weren't in uniforms.

"In La Palude, Mr. Joe," said Matteo, the slighter of the two, "it is not a safe thing to display a Cop's uniform on regular duty. There are exceptions, but for an investigation, plainclothes does suffice."

"Let us transit," put in Lorenzo, who was somewhere between my size and that of the last goon I'd seen. "Work beckons us."

"Sure does," said Denny. The four of us went back to public transit and ended up in La Palude.

Denny and I were dressed in togs that were a little more downscale than our usual duds. I affected a pair of overalls, a white undershirt with no sleeves, well-worn pants, and decently comfortable brogans. The thing I balked about most was trading my fedora for a flat cap. They told me nobody wore that kind of headgear down there, so I reluctantly complied.

As for my partner, Denny got rid of his business suit and wound up in a white shirt, dark brown pants, and black shoes that weren't quite shined. He insisted on getting a mustache, but we made him take off his damned bow tie. He was the picture of a denizen trying to get out of the Swamp. Sadly, it took more than a better suit to do that.

Both of us had remodeled our facial features somewhat, but if we could pass as anything but American Sector guys, it would be a miracle from Gates.

The Swamp itself, well, wasn't much to look at. Homes and buildings that, thanks to lack of credits, were decaying. Low-level places of employment.

A bar and a church on just about every block. He-comps and she-comps drifting by with looks that had gone past desperation to acceptance. The Deeps was more threatening, but the Swamp was more depressing.

Matteo said, sotto voce, "You are a worker in a factory that makes ChipAides, for the young folk. Your partner is your nephew, who works in the firm's office but wishes to upgrade his fortunes. Neither of you is from around here."

"You can say that again," Denny agreed. "But don't."

Our cover names had already been given to us. It took awhile, but Matteo steered us towards a medium-sized Church of Gates. "Why not a bar, Matteo?" I asked him.

Lorenzo answered me. "Don't you know that churches can answer questions, too?"

I looked at Denny, who looked back at me. "Lead on," I said.

We went through a small door on the front left of the church and found ourselves in a small reception area, with a big glorified picture of Gates smiling at us benevolently. Under it were the words:

I DON'T THINK THERE'S ANYTHING UNIQUE ABOUT HUMAN INTELLIGENCE.

A motto to live by.

Matteo stuck his fingers against the plate on the right wall. "Short audience with the priest on call. Blessings."

"Blessings returned," said the speaker beneath the plate.

Denny folded his arms and fidgeted a bit. "I haven't been in a church in a long time."

Matteo and Lorenzo both gave him a curious look. "You wouldn't be an agnostic, would you?" I asked.

"No, I can't believe the cyberverse just happened. It's just hard for me to think that Ops were smart enough to build it."

Matteo snorted. "There are Ops and Ops, my friend. Have faith in what you do not know."

"I'll try," Denny said.

"All will someday be known," Lorenzo said, reverently.

I sighed again, leaned against the wall, closed my eyes, and prayed fervently that Gates would send one of his Messengers to tell me where Alice was, and that she was still alive.

"Brethren?"

I opened my eyes. That was a new voice.

A priest was before us. He was a bit shorter than me, in a black cassock with the symbol of Gates on a chain about his neck. His hair was white and a bit puffy, he had blue eyes and a nose so big I could almost ride on it, and his hands were clasped before him and looked scarred in a few places. I guessed this priest had dusted a few bad guys' jaws in times past. Scars could be demanifested. If you chose to show them, it was a challenge.

"Frater Jonas, my name is Matteo," our pard said, his hand open in greeting. "The large one is my friend Lorenzo. These others are my new friends, Giuseppe and Diego. We seek your typical wise counsel."

The priest laughed lightly at that. "Take care when you ask a priest for counsel, brother. Though we wear the Name, our RAM and ROM are often as dumb as yours."

For some reason, we all laughed, genuinely. It probably had something to do with the relief of tension. I could like this priest, if I had time.

"Though, as the Church says, all things are spiritual, Frater, we come for advice respecting a more cyber-bound matter," Matteo explained. "I have heard that your finger is on the pulse of the sector."

"Even my thumb is not that big, Matteo," said Jonas. "But say on."

"Giuseppe's nephew, Diego, wishes to seek his fortune in a bigger sector, but he must leave secretly," said Matteo. "He is indentured to his place of employment for another 100 cycles. Diego is wise but wishes not to waste any more of his youth in this place."

The priest stroked his chin. "And you think I have knowledge of secret paths?"

Lorenzo spoke up. "We cannot know, Frater, unless we ask."

Frater Jonas gave me the eye. "They say you are this unit's uncle. Is this true?"

I thought twice about lying, then I answered, "He is like a nephew to me, Frater. Though he works in the firm's office, we have bonded and I give him a room to live in. For me, he is like the son I never had."

That last bit was more honest than I wanted to admit. Matteo and Lorenzo gave me some sideways looks that said: Don't screw this up, you.

"Will you not be suspect when he is not present at work?" the priest asked.

"I am an older unit. His life is before him. That which is his, is now behind me."

Jonas sized me up and, thankfully, nodded. Then he turned to Denny. "May I hear from you, Diego?"

"You may, Frater," his manner was respectful, almost reverent.

"Is what these others have told me true?"

"It is true, Frater. I wish to leave the Swamp."

The priest took his time about answering. "If I give you info, it may bind you for more than 100 cycles, brother-son. Those who could provide such a service ask not for time, but money."

"We have money," Denny said.

"They ask many credits," said Jonas.

"We have money," Denny repeated.

The priest shook his head. "Dare I add another sin to my record? If I do, Diego, you must take a binding from me, as well."

Denny hesitated. I nodded at him, and he nodded to Jonas.

"Agreed, Frater."

"Have you been Inducted, my son?" inquired the priest very seriously.

After a moment, Denny shook his head.

"Are you ready to be Inducted, my son, into the Faith?"

"I am, Frater. If you will induct me yourself."

The priest smiled and offered his hand. Denny took it, and Jonas led him past a concealment wall that parted for them. The kid gave a last glance back at me, and I tried to give him a reassuring one of my own. Then they were gone.

Induction was very private.

The three of us were left alone. Matteo, breaking the silence, said, "When were you Inducted, Giuseppe?"

"When I was a chip," I replied truthfully.

"Is your faith still great?"

"Oh, yes. Has to be."

We heard a few groans of emotion and what might have been crying, despite the walls between, and Jonas's voice rising in a chant I didn't understand, before it all became unintelligible again. I could have recorded it and analyzed it later, but would never think of doing that.

Some minutes later, the Frater emerged from the wall again. He was supporting Denny in what was roughly a fireman's carry. Denny was, indeed, crying.

"The Induction is made," the priest beamed. "He is now of the Faith of Gates."

"Bless you, Frater," said Denny thru his tears. "Bless you."

I wanted to ask the priest about a blessing for my quest, and for Alice. Also, I wanted to hole Denny up in a hotel while he was still recovering from his emotional storm. Not being able to do either of those things, I made preps to go to the place Frater Jonas had told us about.

As the four of us hoofed it out, a safe enough distance away from the Church (if the Frater didn't have listening devices trained on us), I braced Denny. "Do you really think you're up to the next phase of this business, Den?"

Lorenzo and Matteo looked at the both of us as Denny said, "Absolutely, Joe. Now more than ever. Gates is with me."

"Good, in that case…"

I slapped the hell out of him in one stroke. The kid cried out. Lorenzo was about to come at me but Matteo held him back.

"Joe, what was that for?" Denny was holding his cheek, looking at me like I was a hippogriff or something.

"That, was to bust the tears out of you. I know what a conversion experience is like, kid. Trust me. Glad you had it. But bawling like a new-minted chip won't help us in this next part. Are you in or are you out, kid? Say it like you mean it.'

"I mean it, J…" he got out, yelling, before I covered his mouth with my hand.

"Shhh. Now I'm going to take my hand away. What is my name, kid?"

I lifted my hand from his mouth and he said, "Giuseppe, sir."

"Exactly. You yelling anything else would not be such a good idea in this neighborhood."

"I agree," said Matteo. "We are in circumstances I would prefer to be out of. But remember the Faith, Diego, and let it aid you." He touched his forehead with his palm, and Denny, possibly for the first time, returned the gesture.

"We should go to our destination," said Lorenzo. "Or do you wish to wait a night, Mr. Giuseppe?"

"I can't afford to wait," I said. "Let's pick it up, guys."

⋟–⋞

Said destination was a three-story place that looked like it had seen its better days when somebody was thinking up radar. The manifestations of wood-and-glass windows and soiled stucco, coupled with a roof of Spanish-style shingles, half of which were cracked and the other half barely hanging on, gave me no confidence that we weren't being conned. But I'd been conned before, and had some interesting experiences in the process.

"That's where we're going?" Denny sounded more like his old self.

"Yes, Diego," Matteo told him. "Once again, Lorenzo and I will make introductions."

I noticed a couple of guys across the street eyeing us. I turned my head and gave them an eye back, and they went back to doing nothing.

We stepped past substance in the shape of a wrought-iron fence, passed over a wilting garden, and advanced to the house proper. The outside plate was a bit rusty. Matteo touched it and a voice said, "Who?"

"My name is Matteo. We have been sent here by Frater Jonas. My young friend bears his token."

"Why?"

"We wish to enquire into transport."

"Where?"

"To be discussed with your padron," Matteo said, somewhat impatiently.

The door beside the plate retracted to the right. A guy larger than Lorenzo piled out of it. He must have had two power units working overtime to maintain his outfit.

"We require identification. And scanning."

Each of us handed over what passed for ID's. I hoped the ones the Cops provided were as good as what the Ring could have done. Denny also handed over a coin he had received from the priest. The behemoth, probably smarter than his size belied, studied them both, then slapped the plate outside with a mitt the size of an Earth whale's fin.

Reddish light played over us from a projector just underneath the shingles, thin as a laser but broad enough to cover us all. It made me squint as it analyzed us from crania to feet. I glanced at the other three, who seemed nervous. For this locale, that was entirely appropriate.

The huge man stepped away from the door and jerked his thumb towards it. "You will enter."

Saying nothing, we did. Matteo was first, I followed him, Denny was after me, and Lorenzo took up the tail position.

Our mountainous acquaintance came last of all and the door schussed shut behind him. For our part, we weren't paying him that much attention. The interior of the place held all our eyes.

It was a damn palace.

Marbleish walls of white and gold, a floor just the same with an inlaid map of the Sicilian sector interwoven in what looked like platinum, objects of art either copied from priceless ones in the Op world or styled by what had to be the highest-priced artists in the Community. Bookshelves of fake oak, with codex books representing ancient texts, but which would probably communicate like data disks if you opened them. The cries of rare birds not far off, and the sound of what had to be water splashing into whatever received it.

Plus incredibly tough-looking guards, two by two, standing against the walls at regular intervals and examining us like viruses they'd be pleased to eradicate. They were armed. Some of the weaponry I knew of, some of it I didn't.

On the inside, this fellow lived large.

One of the guard detatched himself, slung, or rather, attached his weapon to his back, and looked up at the megabeing following us.

"Scanned, Georgio?"

"Yes," said the behemoth.

"Identified?"

"Yes. From the priest."

The guard finally looked at us. "Follow me."

We probably each looked at each other before we did.

Sandwiched between the guard and Georgio, we walked on through more architectural beauty until we came to a central place. It was circular, with solar beams filtering through a semitransparent roof. The columns were white, probably in ancient Roman style, though I didn't feel like checking my data bank. As for the floor, it seemed like platinum veined by gold, and I blanched at the idea of putting my feet on it. But I did.

In the very center of it was a pool, several meters in diameter. At one side, a female figure held a jug, and from that jug poured water, splashing into said pool. At another end, a large fish held open its mouth, draining away the overflow. Birds of various hues and types flew near the ceiling, singing their singular songs, and luckily dropped nothing on us.

In the pool was a fat man whose arms still showed muscularity. His facial shape seemed to be a compromise between a sphere and a block, and though his hair was stylishly grey to reflect age and experience, his mustache was large and black. So were his eyebrows, and his eyes, brown and deep, conveyed little geniality. But he turned his head to look at us, and displayed a smile of large white teeth.

As for the rest of him, he had a large belly and kinda short legs, and was naked. The water covered him from his navel down.

THE WATER COVERED HIM FROM HIS NAVEL DOWN.

I shouldn't neglect the fact that there were a bunch more guards lining the walls, all in the dark green uniform their kind were apparently issued.

"Gabriel, my friend," the naked man boomed, "what have you brought to me today?"

The guard, bowing his head a bit. "Four, sir, with the coin of Jonas."

The four of us kept silent. The man in the pool rubbed his chin briefly, then turned to Georgio the defiler of the inverse-square law. "Why are they here?"

"Transit, they say, sir," Georgio said.

The man turned to Gabriel and nodded towards the doorway. "To your post," he commanded. The guard saluted, turned crisply, and marched out of the room.

As he did so, I saw the eyes of the woman holding the water pitcher glance towards him. I hope I suppressed a reaction, but it wasn't easy. The woman was a living unit.

Was the water being channeled through her pitcher, or through her?

Leaning against the side of the pool casually, the man said, "I am Arturo. It is well you have the Frater's coin. Else, you would either be eating dirt with your faces in my yard outside, or you would be under it. Tell me of yourselves, and why you have come to me."

And before any of us could answer, he changed his features into that of a horned, red-hued demon with teeth I don't even want to re-image, and bellowed one word:

"NOW."

Sure, I was shocked at first. So were all of us. I had a feeling the guards along the walls were a bit, too, but they probably suppressed showing it. After that moment passed, I had another distinct reaction.

And I decided to do something about it.

Matteo started in with his shpiel. "Don Arturo, we have come to you for…"

"Shut it," I held my hand up for silence.

My consigliore, so to speak, had his mouth open like a fish. Lorenzo and Denny, whom I checked, looked even more unbelieving than when the Don had shown his demon-face. The guards, if anything, were even more alert.

Arturo, still half-covered with water, had his eyes opened to an extent an oculist wouldn't think possible.

"Let me show you who I am," I manifested my features and clothes back to their natural state. I even managed to reshape my cap into a serviceable fedora. And I looked the Don right in his twice-normal-size eyes.

"My name is Joe. I'm a P.I. We didn't come here to trap you or bring you in. But I have a quest for a missing woman, and I need your help."

Arturo sat up with a look of fury, hands grabbing the pool's edge. "I will Crash you for this, Giorgio! You say you scanned this man? I will Crash you and your entire family!"

Lorenzo and Matteo had cycled their coloration involuntarily to whiteness. But Denny just looked grim and ready. Good for him.

"Don't worry about him, Don Arturo," I said. "Talk to me. Someone not of your brotherhood took a woman from me. I would find her, find him, and Crash him."

"I will Crash you all!" he yelled. "Priest's coin or no coin, no Cop invades the home of Arturo! GUARDS!"

That was when I walked up to him and slapped him in the face.

The Don grabbed the side of the face that I'd slapped and tried to balloon his eyes out even further than before.

"That's a challenge, Arturo, unless you're too weak in the circuits to accept it. Back where I come from, the big boys don't have to hide behind a double score of mooks. To stay where they are, they've got to take on their rivals themselves."

Arturo doubled the hand that had caressed his cheek into a fist. "Set your stakes," he hissed.

"This. We fight unit y unit. If I win, you tell me who used your transit to take my woman, and tell me where I can find him. I demand that."

"And if I win?" the Don loaded a mountain of hate between his words.

"Then all four of us die. You will Crash us all."

"No!" Matteo shouted.

Denny intervened. "Shut up. Joe knows. It's the only way."

Arturo and I stared each other down for an eternity. It was broken by Denny, who stood beside me and looked at the Don with the most perfect expression of righteous anger I've seen to this day.

"You betray Gates," he accused. "And if my friend loses, I will Crash you before I die."

Arturo broke the stare and almost smiled. "Your pup shows spirit. But if Gates has not allowed me to prosper, if Gates has not given me the power I have, who then?"

"Wozniak," said Denny in a quiet snarl.

That's when the fight started.

The Don roared out of his pool, literally, expanding his face again into that of a demon, but making it much huger and with more teeth. The rest of him was nude and dripping but I didn't have time to appreciate it. I shortened myself to duck him and clamped both my hands together, turning them into a rough version of a miner's hammer, and slammed him hard against the side of his head. He looked a bit hurt, but so were my hands.

I tumbled him out of the pool and onto the floor, his bulk helping somewhat. He ended up on bottom, and I re-formed one of my arms into a sword and tried to plunge it into his gut. Said sword ended up caught between two hands formed into cross-swords. Arturo was hardly an amateur. He kicked me in the gut the way an Opworld mule must kick, and I planed back into the pool. There was a big splash and the water felt great, but it wasn't time to appreciate that.

In a trice, the Don was on me, using substance of his belly to manifest eight flexible arms like that of an octopus. He drew me closer, both of us underwater but, unlike Ops, unable to drown, and opened his horrendous jaws to deface my face. With a little quick thinking, I reformed my head into a round column and slammed it between his jaws, hitting him in the back of his throat. Then I retracted my head before his jaws could snap shut, but I still noted a substance leak at my forehead. I sent a crusher kick into his abdomen and pushed him away.

I sprang out of the pool, out of the water, and rolled over to a side opposite my three compadres. The noise of yelling, probably both from them and the guards, and the pitcher-maid for all I knew, was audible. But I got my very damp-and-cold body into a fighting stance and kept my eye on my opponent.

Arturo should have won an award for his innovative battle techniques. His two arms shifted into bunches of tendrils with deadly ripping claws at the ends of them. They sprang towards me and, from the tears in my clothes and the stinging in my body; I could tell they were doing the job.

So was I. My arms formed synapse-quickly into twin fan-blades that sheared off Arturo's claw-tendrils and sent them flying to the edges of the pool. My brothers-in-chips and the guards all backed off like data from the Black Virus. He couldn't connect to those weapons until the fight was over. He'd lost substance, and if he lost enough, I might win this fight.

With that in mind, I gave him an axe-blow with an arm literally shaped like an axe, right to the neck. It left a gap you could see through, starting at the edge and going just under his Adam's apple. Not enough to Crash him. That would take a blow straight thru the middle of his head, from the top (or, if you pushed up enough, from the bottom). But it did damage.

Unfortunately, about that time, he clamped two vise-hands around my left calf and tore off my foot and lower leg.

I screamed, but I didn't let it stop me.

The Don was trying to brain me with my own leg. It hurt like a sonofawoz and I was patching up a scab across the wound to try and stop the substance leak. While I did that, I formed my upper part into a drill, aimed carefully, and laid waste to his gut. The scream I heard was one of the sweetest sounds this side of Alice's sighs.

I managed to thrust my whole body thru him, came out on the other side, grabbed my leg from him, and bashed him over the head with it to let him know how it felt. In this fight, I had the disadvantage of not being able to Crash him, since I needed his info. But he had no such problem with me.

We smashed into each other again and again. I didn't have time to reattach my leg. We were both leaking like a target that had been drilled by a 30-beam projector. He bit me and I bit him. Sometimes, it got hard to tell if we were biting each other or ourselves.

The Don made most of his remaining self into a mallet and smashed me and I fell on the floor like a beached stingray.

Through my good old slitted optics I saw him reform himself, join both arms at the elbows, form them into an axe, and rear back.

I formed my own arm into a battle-axe, swung towards the side of Arturo's neck that was unsevered, and cut the matrixless plugger's head off.

Arturo's head fell and bounced on the floor, causing him to yelp in pain. His body, off-balance and on the edge of the pool, hesitated an instant and fell backwards with a satisfying splash.

The distance between myself and his head could probably have been measured in light years, but I made it.

My arm was still a battle-axe, and Arturo saw it was hanging over the middle of his head. Even the guards didn't move.

"Tell me now," I rasped. "Tell me now, or you Crash with me."

He sighed, possibly in pain, possibly in disappointment, but I didn't care which.

"The Deepest Deeps," he said. "The transit relay. From the Deepest Deeps."

⋛-⋜

We managed to baste my leg back onto its base until I could get medical attention. I held onto Arturo's head, as it was the only way we could get out of there safely. The soldiers insisted one of them would accompany us, and Gabriel got the honors. Denny's arm was formed into a deadly cutting instrument, and it was clear he'd Crash Arturo if anyone gave us grief. Lorenzo held my shoulders and Matteo took my feet, and with Gabriel marching beside us, that's how we got out of there.

"Santa Babbagia!" Arturo screamed. "My body will die, you pig!"

"Your body," Denny responded clinically, "should be good for another 25 cycles. We should have you back on it within that time."

"You arrogant pup, you—"

"Shut up," Denny snapped. The Don gave up and closed his mouth.

As we neared the public transit terminal, Gabriel said, "Of course, I will come with you."

"Of course, you will not, unless you wish to spend many cycles in Captivity," answered Matteo.

Gabriel looked almost frantic. "But I must protect my Don!"

"Your Don will get all the protection he needs," I said. "Once we're safe, we'll send him back to you. Right here. Be waiting."

"You unmatrixed..." started Arturo, and then gave up. It wasn't worth the effort. I had him held by the hair, in my right hand. His neck-stump was only inches from the ground. I gave him a shake and he went "Arrrr" or something equivalent.

"We're not going to take you in, Arturo. Once we're safe, you're coming back here, and Gabe can see about getting the best doctors around to reunite you with your beloved body."

"I will have you Crashed, spawn of a pig and a Timex! You and all three others of you."

"I don't think so. Info travels fast in these parts. Even you have rivals. Once they hear about what happened to you today, you'll probably spend all your time trying to keep them from taking over your turf."

Arturo made a sound. He knew it was true.

"Perhaps we can make a deal," he offered. "If you keep silent about this—incident, I vow you and your company have nothing to fear from me. It would, as you say, affect my reputation."

I raised my head to look at Denny, Lorenzo, Gabriel, and the back of Matteo's head.

"I think I can speak for us all, except Gabriel here. He should know better than to squeal. For us, if we stay safe from harm, we'll keep quiet."

After a pause, Arturo said, "Agreed."

I told Gabriel, "Wait here till we send him back."

Then we manifested on the next transit and left.

⇒–⇐

As soon as we reached Cop Central, I had myself carried into the Chief's office, displayed Arturo's head, who responded with a snarl, and told him about the bargain. The Chief looked mighty disappointed. "You bring me the greatest find in the entire city, and expect to let him go? Without a single question?"

"We made a bargain. Want to see if he violates it if you don't go along?"

The Chief gave me a disgusted look and then bent and gave Arturo a nastier one. "Later."

"In your nightmares, Cop," Arturo replied.

Motioning to an aide, the Chief said, "Put him in a protective box. Label it. Send it back to where he came from."

"Right away, Chief," said the young Cop, and took Arturo away from me. He was swinging the head in a circle and whistling as he walked away.

"I wouldn't send that kid anywhere near the Swamp if I were you," I opined.

"As if that would make a difference," the Chief replied.

⇒–⇐

None of us thought that Denny and I remaining in the Sicilian Sector any longer was a great idea. We caught the fastest transit out of there and, of necessity, manifested within Norton's clinic. The Norton. He took a look at me and almost cried with frustration.

"For the love of Gates, Joe, why? Why?"

I shrugged. "Tried ballroom dancing and my partner didn't think much of my technique."

Norton indulged in some of the most creative swearing I've ever heard. Then he pulled up a gurney, floated it about a foot off the floor, and lay me on it. He removed my hat and hung it on a hook set into the wall, possibly for just that purpose. Then he turned to Denny. "Out," he said.

"Sorry, sir. Where Joe goes, I…"

"OUT."

Denny outed.

⇒–⇐

I suppose I dreamed when Norton put me under deep sleep cycle. It's just that I have no idea what it was about. Maybe my memory bank had been through enough trauma itself that it didn't feel like constructing any grand epics for me to enjoy while Norton fiddled with my leg and other hurt places.

We all need a break sometimes. Me, I suppose I had quite a few of them.

When Norton and whatever helper-elves he worked with were finally done, and they had some belief that I wouldn't jump up and start voiding substance thru a large wound in my stomach, they put me to bed and let me sleep more of it off. I'm pretty sure Denny was there for my initial convalescence. There were nicely colored growth crystals in a vase beside my bed, and that would have been just like him.

But when I awoke, he wasn't the one I saw beside me.

"Afternoon, Joe," said Kelly, with his very tight smile.

"Hi, Kelly," I managed to say. "Afternoon of what?"

"Norton told me to wait till he tells you that," Kelly answered. "I agreed. You look like you went ten rounds with an ancient punch-card puncher."

"Shoulda seen the other guy, Kelly."

"I heard about him. You've been into hell so many times they must have a seat reserved for you there."

"With the biggest Expander you ever seen. Trust me."

He looked away, then back at me. "Joe, here's how it is. The Ring is starting to think that this business you're in is large enough for them to take notice."

I probably smiled. I know I yawned. "Bless 'em, Kelly. They really stay on top of things, don't they?"

"More often than not, we follow you to find out where things are," Kelly admitted. He wasn't smiling. "The situation is, Joe, they've reinstated your privileges. Where you go now, you'll have Ring support."

I nodded. "Nice to know." I meant it and he knew I did.

Kelly took something from his pocket and held it up so I could see it. "This is yours. Again."

A Ring tracker.

I put it on my wrist. "Thanks, Kelly. Does Denny get one, too?"

"He's got one," Kelly confirmed. After a moment, he continued. "Where do we stand now, Joe? What's the situation?"

"I know a little more about where to take this, Kelly. But nobody's handling it without me on point. And way out in front."

"You might be a couple more weeks in here."

"That'll be a nice vacation, then. Unless you can push Norton to get me out of here faster."

Kelly seemed very tired. Then he shook his head and laughed. "You, Joe. You're the most incorrigible matrixless son of a you-know-what I have ever encountered in my entire measured existence."

"I'll bet you say that to all the half-dead P.I.'s," I smiled.

But in the back of my banks, a few bits and bytes were trying to make connections.

I hadn't formed a full theoretical matrix yet, but I was getting a few notions as to how this whole thing might end.

And I didn't know what to think of it.

It took me a good couple of weeks to heal up, just as predicted. Denny was in to see me just about as soon as Kelly left, and they got him a simbed to sleep in when he was in my room. Which, of course, was most of the time. I loved the kid for it.

Kelly visited a couple more times, of course, and kind of bonded with Denny. That was nice. Even Norton came by, beyond his usual rounds, and we settled up to a few comfy games of Pac-Man and Splash the Ship, among others. I didn't feel like wasting my credits at Online Poker, and neither, thankfully, did Norton.

"You've got the luck of Gates on you, Joe," said Norton, and I saw Denny nodding in the background.

"Gonna need it," I confirmed, and kept playing.

Denny kept noodging me for more info on what was next, and I told him he'd find out when the time was right. I fed him war stories, and he loved those. Thinking of him as a son, even unadopted, was getting easier and easier.

What was getting harder was the thought of throwing him into the next phase of our operation. I wasn't hot on throwing myself in there, either. But having him survive left open the chance of someone carrying on after this. The kid was as green as the go signal on a traffic light, but he was turning redder all the time, so to speak. No yellow in his makeup that I could see.

Meantime, I had to hope my adversary would be patient enough to wait for me. I figured he would, because this, simply put, was a strike at me. If he wanted an enemy worth fighting, he'd have to cool his heels for a time.

A trap isn't worth anything if you can't get your quarry to step into it.

Like it or not, I was going to have to step right into that thing as quickly as I could, and maybe feel its teeth snap shut on my precious thigh.

And where he was, I couldn't count on Norton to come save me.

But the point was: Alice was down there too. Gates only knew what he'd done to her. What he was doing to her.

That meant I'd be packing my bags for hell, on the double.

⇒-⇐

The evening of the day I got out of the hospital, I was still using a CyberCane so as not to put too much mass on my recently reattached leg. Denny hovered near me, from the doors of Norton Land thru the transit to my place, and inside. He had everything the doc had given me to get me thru, and he knew not to let me nudge the pain blocks for two more days.

I was sitting in my most comfortable chair, cane wedged between it and my right leg, with the lights low and the best sound distorters the Ring could give me making sure Denny and I had privacy. My partner sat across from me, having manifested a white T-shirt, maroon pants, and no shoes. At least he didn't have his bow tie on. I let the atmosphere cool a bit before I spoke.

"Den, I've figured out who's stringing us," I confessed. "It came together for me when I was in the hospital. I'm going to give it to you, but you've got to make your decision when the story's done, not before."

"The decision, Joe, is…"

I sighed. "Do I have to keep cutting you off, Denny? I said when it's done, and not before. Are your audions on right?"

"Sorry, Joe. Go ahead."

"It goes back a few good cycles, and it's another Ring case. The hardest one I ever got. Worse than the Sicilian, worse than any of the ones I've told you about. This one I've held back."

The kid's elbows were on his knees and his fists supported his head. His eyes didn't leave my face.

"The Ring got word that someone from the Deeps was planning a big strike on the Op World," I continued. "They assigned me to find out who it was and take care of it. I had to go undercover, just like I did in the last sector. Only this time it was a lot tougher. I'll spare you the details. The bit was, the guy responsible was a unit named—Henry.

"Henry might have called himself an anarchist, I don't know. I got into his confidence and he told me he was sick of Ops dumping us every time they found a unit with more goodies. He said he was going to paralyze the Ops by spreading a code that would deactivate all nuclear weapons. See where I'm going with this? Henry thought big. He said he'd broadcast an ultimatum to our good old controllers and force them to keep us active, or lose their precious activation codes forever. Also, Henry had mastered the art of body transfer. He could upload his consciousness into a unit. If, of course, he murdered the unit beforehand."

"And—he had?"

I gave him a nod. "But the codes he'd stolen weren't deactivation codes, Denny. They were activation codes. Henry was gonna start nuclear war in the Op world, and finish it too. All of that while he uploaded himself into a Mars probe, from which he'd come down later, once the dust quit bouncing. He said it'd be his world then, and he'd make it into whatever he pleased.

"There was also a fem unit called Nina. She was my first love, Denny. Her address at the time was in the Deeps. It'd been a long time between meetings for us, and don't ask me what she was doing there. But we started things up again, and...and..."

The kid was at my side, touching my shoulder. "It's okay, Joe. It's really okay."

"Oh, Woz, it was anything but okay! The woman got word to the Ring, and Henry...the matrixless, plugless sonofawoz smashed her. He smashed her."

The only noise for a good long while was the hum of the temp regulators.

"Joe, go on."

I had to. Didn't want to.

"It took me and all of Henry's top guys to put him down. Henry crashed one of them, bad nasty. The only way to stop him was to shove him into the Deepness. You know about it, that hellpit that nobody's ever been thru and come back to tell it. One of his men gave his existence to get him down in there. We all figured that was it. Nina got a new programmed identity after they put her back together again. The woman I loved, she's gone."

After a pause, Denny uttered, "The Deepest Deeps. That's where Arturo said the relay came from."

"Probably not directly. But this all fits. The Deepness, snatching Alice—he couldn't bait me with Nina anymore, but he could with Alice. Since a woman I loved stopped him last time..."

"He's using another woman you love to draw you to your death."

"Yeah." The thought about trying to move a pain block or two on my leg crossed my mind. I let it go its merry way.

"So, Den, now it's After."

He didn't smile. "You know what my answer is."

"I gave you a choice," I told him and then I clapped him on the arm. "Make yourself useful, son. Get hold of three guys for me, if it's not too late and we can still find 'em. I'll tell you what to say."

"Yo-hey, sir," said the unit who'd been Sixties Guy. He grinned at me and saluted, standing on my doorstep.

"Come on in, and tell me your name," I stood aside for him. "We didn't get acquainted like that last time."

"I'm Chuck," he pumped my hand. He was blonde, he had a regular haircut, and he was wearing a white suit and sneakers. "Not much of a name for an ex-hippie, but you know how it goes."

"I do indeed." With a hand on his shoulder, I guided him into the living room. Three others were already sitting there.

Marlon, the former Jungle Guy, kept his black hair long and was physically his former size, but he had a dark green business suit manifested. He jumped up and greeted Chuck with a smile. Percy, aka Mr. Pin-Stripe, had on a black blazer, an orange pullover shirt, and black pants. His hair was light brown and even though he smiled, he looked like he was all business. My partner was sitting backwards in a kitchen chair.

"Marlon and Percy you already know. This is my partner Denny. Denny, this is Chuck, who used to be as Sixties as the Grateful Dead."

"Why were they grateful?" murmured Denny.

"Skip it. Have a seat, Chuck, and listen to my shpiel." Chuck obeyed, seating himself between his two comrades.

"Okay if we have a moment of silence for our two fallen partners?" said Marlon.

"Fine by me." We measured off a minute for the Soldier and Guy Fawkes.

After that, I went on. "I've got a problem that's bleeding over into the whole Community. Henry isn't dead."

Silence.

"How do you know?" asked Percy.

I gave them the high points of our case. "We all thought the Deepness would kill him," I finished. "Apparently it didn't."

"How, how about Guy?" said Chuck. "You know, Guy Fawkes. He jumped on top of him and went down with him."

"No intel on that yet," Denny said. "It's QED."

I clenched my hands, twiddled my thumbs. "If Henry's alive, I'm hoping Alice is alive. Don't know about Guy. But Henry's activity indicates that, yes, the Deepness can be survived."

"Nobody's ever come back from there yet," Marlon pointed out. "Plus, Henry had more power than any single comp."

"He did, and he may have more now," I ssuggested. "Or less. But as long as he's got Alice down there, I'm going after him."

"With some help from the Ring," Denny put in. "Joe's already ordered equipment."

Percy worked his jaw and then said, "You've ordered us, too."

"Yep, I have," I said, and gave them time to sort it out. Then I went on.

"You three guys knew Henry longer than I did. Maybe you have a better handle on his nature, even though I learned a lot about him in my time. If Henry's calling me out, it's gotta be bigger than just a revenge plot. He's a megalomaniac. There's got to be something else back of this."

"How about the activation codes?" said Marlon. "For the nukes, I mean."

"The codes were changed after that incident," Denny reported. "He won't be able to use that trick again."

"Bringing it back to the table, gents," I continued, "I've got no right to tell you to help out on this. You've made lives for yourselves in the Community. The most logical step would be for you to go back to them. Only—if we don't get him this time, in the near future there might not be a Community, or Henry just might be calling the shots. We don't know. But we know his character.

"So if you want to walk out the door, nobody's blaming you. Transit out of here and be safe, for the moment. But I sure could use your help, guys. It's up to you."

It didn't take very long for Marlon to say, "I'm in."

Chuck shook his head. "Just get this damn thing done before the wife has a chance to complain. Okay, Joe?"

Percy, formerly a faux mobster, declared, "I don't want to do it."

I shrugged, and I think I saw Denny do the same.

"That doesn't mean I'm not gonna do it," Percy clarified. "Just I don't want to. Where do we go from here?"

>-<

Where we went was up to the Ring, courtesy of Kelly. I wasn't going to be alone on this, nor were the other four. We were the spearhead of the operation.

Our quintet was outfitted with protective suits that would have looked appropriate in an Op science fiction vid. They were form-fitting but insulated, complete with helmets and impulse drives to move us around. We also had communicators in said helmets, and weapons with which we hoped we wouldn't Crash our own heads in. The trainer boys gave us a brief course on how to use them, but I still wasn't confident.

Kelly regarded the white-suited bunch of us in the prep room. "We'll be tracking you all, of course, and the feeds in your helmets will give us a pretty good readout of your surroundings. No existing unit has ever made it back from that place. Whatever the case, we want a better picture of it in case we have to go back again."

Not a man of us missed the implication thereof. I had somehow morphed from a private detective into a sergeant, leading troops into battle. That was not a comforting thought.

"We'll have troops massed, waiting to go in," Kelly said. "But we'll be waiting to see how it goes for you. If we want to pull the abductee out alive, or, as you three pointed out, your lost team member, a small unit is better for that. I hate to say you're going in blind, but you damned well are."

After that, he said, "All right, gentlemen. Let's get started."

>-<

I doubt the citizens of the Deeps were prepared for the sight of five men in protective suits materializing from the transit station. A few folks were lined up, waiting to go wherever they went, and they were bowled over when they saw us. We excused ourselves the best we could, and trudged on. Kelly and his men weren't far behind.

We weren't expecting the round of applause we got. Evidently the hoi polloi of the Deeps were glad to see some law enforcement after too long a time without it. Hopefully, Kelly took note.

The guards that he brought down with him helped keep the forming crowds back from us. Someone threw something at us and it pinged off Denny's helmet. He tried to find out who'd thrown it, but I shook my head at him. He continued on.

Nobody really impeded us. The folk of the Deeps, male and female, were curious to see what was coming off. Well, so were we, in another

THEY WERE BOWLED OVER WHEN THEY SAW US.

fashion. I tried to keep the pace fairly brisk so as to dampen down the little voice in my RAM that told me to turn around and get the hell out of there.

After a few more blocks, all of us were near the Deepness.

A wall of energy had been placed around it to keep looky-lous from falling into it since our last encounter with Henry. Our pal Kelly went to a control box, keyed it open, and made a door-gap for us. The five of us went in and stood on the edge of the ground before that circular spot of varying colors and hypnotic pulsing. I looked at the others and tried reading their faces thru the dimmed plates.

None of them exactly looked eager.

I drew a long pseudo-breath. "After me, fellas. Mark One."

Then I closed my eyes and jumped.

Before I opened them, I felt a hellacious pressure drop and heard a tremendous thrumming noise. My hand went to my audio control and adjusted it down, automatically. My team's PM's would come through without problems. Then I forced my optics open.

The scenario was that of a rainbow crossed with magnetic currents crossed with what could have been the fourth or fifth dimension trying to break in. For all I knew, it was. And I was falling. Gates only knew how I knew it, but I was falling.

Was this a gateway, a warp to another world? Maybe the Op World itself? Or was it just the outside of Hell?

Didn't matter.

"This is Unit One, repeat, Unit One," I said in a broad PM. "Talk to me, guys."

"Unit Two," said Denny. "Repeat, Unit Two. I'm here."

Chuck said, "Unit Four. Can you read me?"

Percy answered, "Roger that, Unit Four. This is Five."

"And this is Three," said Marlon. "Too late to go back for lunch?"

"Plus X on that, Three," I said. "Keep your bearings, guys, and watch out for each other."

The 3D locator readout near the bottom of my helmet gave me the positioning of my four neo-soldiers. We were falling at an increasing rate, and the pressure drop was replaced by a pressure increase. The magnetic fields were for real. I could feel my suit trying to balloon out and fought with the wrist controls to keep it together. "Guys, maintain suit integrity," I PM'ed them. "This thing is trying to stretch us." Flexible we might be, but I had a feeling that if we lost control, the impulses would spread us over parsecs.

What the hell was I doing there? I was a P.I. by trade and a sometime agent for the Ring, not a soldier. Not an explorer of unknown phenoms.

The image of my lost secretary filled my mind and I didn't have to ask myself those questions anymore.

I sent a message to Kelly and kept it open to the rest of the crew. "Kelly, Unit One here. What can you tell from our input? Over."

The answer came back with some static. "Unit One, this is Kelly. You're getting harder to read. From what we can figure, you're in the outer edges of a vortex phenomenon. Readings are off the charts. Appears to be a warp, but what kind we still haven't figured out. No warp-holes yet, no solid structures except you guys. Is everyone still all right?"

"Plus One, as far as I can tell. I thought it'd be sucking us down like a GroupTube. Doesn't seem as strong as when we put Henry in it."

"I read you, Unit One," Kelly said. "Could be its energy varies, but that's all chaos theory right now. What do you see? Over."

"What don't I see? Too much visual input, Kelly, and if I didn't have the audible damped way down, it'd sound like the biggest Op heart in creation. I…"

That was as far as I got before a circle of unbelievable darkness opened right in front of me. It started dragging me like I was a ball bearing and it was an electromagnet.

Kelly must have been saying something to me at the time. I couldn't really tell. All I knew was, the black thing swallowed me up.

And I came out on the other side.

⋝－⋜

On that other side, I landed and sprawled face down on what appeared to be a carpeted floor. Being in such a position did not lend itself to self-defense or scoping out my surroundings. Thus, I shoved myself up to my feet as well as I could, given the suit, and looked around.

It was a bedroom. A very nice bedroom, in fact, done in faux-cedar paneling, with a chandelier hanging from a mirrored ceiling. That reminded me, fleetingly, of some establishments I had visited, but they didn't bother with chandeliers.

I registered that in an instant. What really drew my attention was a four-poster bed snugged up against one wall. There was someone in the bed, stark naked, her wrists and ankles bound to the posts by servo bonds.

Alice.

She gave a start when she saw me, and I don't blame her. My face was only dimly visible thru the helmet plate. Since I had the sound dampener turned up, I couldn't hear her scream, but I could see her doing it.

My mighty deductive abilities told me that if she was safe without a helmet here, I might be, too. The sensor readouts in that helmet told me she had a real structure. Alice was not an illusion.

Of course, Henry might have dummied up a really convincing ringer, but the hell with that. I popped the helmet back so it was sitting on my shoulders, and gave Alice a look at my questionably handsome features.

"Joe," she gasped. "Joe!"

I wanted to say something but I couldn't. I just couldn't.

This had to be a trap, but if it was, I'd figure it out as I went. My hand weapon could be set to a cutting beam. I placed it between Alice's wrist and one of her bonds. "Stay still, gorgeous."

That was a hell of an opening statement to her, but that's all I could think of.

The beam opened a parting in the wrist-bond and I cracked it the rest of the way open, burning my gloves somewhat in the process. Alice, thankfully, wasn't hurt. Then I repeated the process with her three other bonds, and she was free.

She embraced me, suit and all, and laid tears on my shoulder in what seemed an unending river of them.

"Oh, Joe...oh, Joe."

If time and circumstance had permitted, I would have lain her back down and plugged her for a whole cycle. But there were a few problems that still bore on us. I freed up one arm, reached back for my helmet control, and sent a broad PM. "Anybody, this is Unit One. Repeat, this is Unit One. Found our abductee. Please respond. Over."

Nothing. Alice raised her head from my shoulder, her eyes still dripping tears. I spoke into the sender again. "Anybody receiving, this is Unit One. I have the abductee. Please respond. Repeat, please respond. Over."

Still nothing. I amped up my tracker and hoped somehow they could hone in on me. Or even triangulate.

After another moment, Alice laid her head against my chest. "Joe, I prayed you'd find me."

"Alice....did he?"

She nodded, grimly. I told myself I'd deplug him with my own hands when we next met.

"Fill me in, baby. Tell me what I've got to know."

Alice shook her head. "I just—I was getting ready for bed and he came out of the wall plate. I had that thing locked and coded, Joe. He shouldn't have, he couldn't..."

"Yes, honey. We're dealing with a thing that knows all the rules, and how to get around them. Go on."

"I screamed bloody murder. Didn't know who he was. He said...he said he was Henry, that you owed him something and I'd help him collect." Alice shivered, turned her head down, and started crying again.

"You can cry, baby, but I still need the info. Let me try something." I took the bedcover, tore a swath of it off at the bottom, and gave it to Alice. She wrapped it around herself and tucked it in at the top. It covered her to just below the knees.

"Thank you, Joe."

"Don't mention it. But tell me quick. I have a feeling he'll be here soonest."

"I tried fighting him, Joe. I tried, honest I did. Should have got to my weapon. But he was too strong. And he hit me, Joe. I went out cold."

Another thing I'd pay that matrixless dump back for when we met again. I squeezed Alice gently.

"When I woke up, I was here. He tied me up like I was when you saw me. And he..." She choked.

"I know what he did. Or I can imagine it. What happened next? Did he say anything about a Big Plan, or what he was going to do to me?"

"He told me...I'm trying to replay it now, hold on...he said he wanted to hurt the Community somehow. Said you'd be part of it, and that I was bait for you."

"Sonofawoz. So far, everything's clickin' his way."

She collapsed in my arms. "He took me more than once, Joe. I...you've got to get me out of here. And you've got to stop him."

"Yeah, but I need to get you out of here, honey, and I need to find him first. Where..."

"Don't bother, Joe," said a new voice. "I found you."

My left hand flipped up my helmet and my right pulled out my weapon from its holster. I knew that voice. It wasn't much of a trick to put my corpus between the speaker and Alice.

Henry stood there, in a black suit that was more of a uniform. "Aren't you even going to say hi?"

I said something that wasn't "Hi" and blasted him.

It went through him without harm and made an impact on the wall behind him, blowing a hole in it.

Henry smiled. "Joe. Really. Do you think I'd expose myself to an attack from you, just like that? This is a projection."

"Project yourself in here right now, you coward, and let's get this done."

"All in good time, Joe," said Henry, simpering as he did it. "Shouldn't I let you know my master plan before I destroy you? I hear that's what all the good villains do in Op fictionals."

"Doesn't matter. Come on and fight!"

"Joe, shut up," he retorted. "I'll come in there when I'm good and ready. Right now, I feel like talking. You feel like listening?"

I felt like killing. But I said nothing.

"Well, there you are, Joe. I've got the floor now. My regards to dear Alice, by the way. I've probably taken her more times than you, now."

Red screens, not summoned voluntarily, filled my optics. Alice called him something even I won't repeat. He chuckled.

"The Deepness almost Crashed me, Joe," Henry said. "But not quite. After the dear, departed associate of mine landed on me, I found a way of drawing on its power. An utter non-energy that allowed me to survive, to rebuild myself. Had to do it by instinct, and for cycles upon cycles I couldn't perceive much of anything besides myself. I was on the verge of being a solipsist, really."

I shook my head, my reasoning coming back whether I wanted it to or not. "You always were. You didn't give a damn about anything but yourself, Henry. That's pretty much the same as saying only the self exists."

"You've become a philosopher in your old age, Joe. I always knew you had potential galore. Problem is, you were never smart enough to access it." He brought his face, projected or not, nearer to me. "That's the difference between you and me."

"There's so many differences between you and him, the whole Community couldn't tally them," said Alice, speaking up in a tone that dripped pure virus.

"Just for that, Alice, you'll get an extra plugging after I'm done with your ex, here," said Henry. "You might even…"

"SHUT UP!" I raged.

I turned from him to Alice for a moment, then turned back to him.

When Henry spoke next, his look wasn't humorous. He had the look of a predator.

"Briefly, Joe: though even I haven't figured it all out yet, the Deepness is something of a conduit between the Op world and ours. I have no idea how long it extends. But I have gathered enough knowledge to actuate a certain signal here. A pulse. It's already been started, and it will reach the Community within a fixed time, though you shouldn't expect me to tell you when. It's akin to the pulse a nuclear device in the world of the Ops would have on us. It'll kill the Community, Joe, down to the last infant chip. In the meantime, I will be safe here, satisfying Alice until I weary of her, and constructing the New Community, one which will surpass the wildest dreams of its predecessors. The new Communitarians will worship me, Joe. I'll be their god."

"Show yourself, damn you! Where are you for real?"

From the wall itself, a fist projected and knocked me spinning.

Within barely enough time to record it, the entire room contracted into a humanoid shape—a familiar one. Alice and I were floating in the Deepness.

"I've been all around you, Joe," Henry laughed. "Let's do it."

Henry formed more tentacles than a mutant octopod and sent them all at me. I blasted away at his center with the hand-weapon and sent Mayday messages into the void. Alice was out there somewhere in the Void, and Gates help her, because I sure couldn't. The big hole I'd blasted in Henry's gut was filling in with substance. My protective suit hampered my flexibility, but I shot at Henry's head. He got a couple of tentacles up, made them into a shield, and had them blasted away. Then he retracted his head into his body.

I used my propulsion system to send me right at him, and I sunk my gloved mitts into what amounted to his chest. Find the head and crash it. Find the head and...

WHAMM.

A blow of something with an edge on it came down on my helmet and cracked it. Had to be two of my rhumba partner's limbs in an axe shape. Another one could split the helmet and the head beneath it. I was getting static over my communicator and flashed on the image of an Op astronaut stranded from his capsule or space station.

Wozniak.

If Henry could survive out there without a suit, maybe I could, too. I blasted away at him repeatedly but he shifted his mass to dodge the charges. It bought me time to pop the helmet and morph myself out of the suit. I probably looked like a snake exiting his burrow. Once I was out, I disconnected the blaster and its power pack from the suit.

The Deepness, for all its visual anarchy, wasn't killing me. My body, clad in an opaque all-over garment, tingled all over. I didn't have any time to record what was causing that. Instead of a thrumming, there was silence.

As silent as Space in the Op world.

Henry was changing himself into something big, ugly, threatening, and frightening. Maybe a huge bird of prey, for psychological impact. It'd take some time. I kicked against my suit and propelled myself towards his beak-like mouth. It was big enough for me to stand on his lower jaw and push up with my hands on his upper one. The edges of said beak were sharp enough to cut my mitts and bleed a little substance into the Deepness. I strove to break his mouth.

The bird-Henry spit me out.

Spinning backwards, I went with an idea I had and morphed myself into a python-like shape. By the time Henry-in-bird-form got to me, I was finished enough with it to wrap myself around him and squeeze really hard. For good measure, I sprouted spikes from my underbelly and made him bleed, too.

The bird formed buzzsaw blades to meet my underbelly and began sawing me in half. I released him and pulled myself together. Henry was closing in, but I could resume my humanoid form in nothing flat. After doing so, I used both hands to aim and blasted him right in the head.

The left side of the bird's head came off and, i suppose, spiraled away. But he hadn't Crashed.

Henry's huge right claw knocked my blaster away and almost took my hand with it. He was remolding himself into human form, too. My power pack, trailing the severed end of the cable that had connected it to the blaster, was sputtering energy sparks.

I heaved it at Henry and got him right in the chest.

The ensuing explosion blasted him apart.

I had a hard time convincing myself I'd seen what I had. His half-head suddenly wasn't wearing a body. Both his wings were flapping into the multicolored jungle. One claw was visible. Staring at the mess, I couldn't believe my luck.

Really, I shouldn't have.

A mass of gaseous stuff emerged from the base of the bird's head, expanded, connected to one wing, then the other, then the floating claw, then the other floating claw which I had not seen. The whole mess of a mass was retracting now, morphing into a humanoid form.

Henry had lost substance, but he was still able to attack.

How he shot himself forward in the void, I'm still uncertain. But he did, and he punched me in the face. Hard.

I kneed him between his legs so effectively that the space between his lower limbs was extended several inches.

We morphed out claws, sank them into each other, drew near, fought, bit, gouged. Every nasty thing we knew went into that fight, and we improvised more than a few moves. If either one of us came out of this functional, I thought, it would be a miracle.

Our heads bobbed, weaved, and retracted as we avoided each other's killing center-blow. We made parts of our bodies, usually our hands, into temporary shields to ward off each other's ax-edged blows. Both of us formed drills and penetrated into each other's guts. Neither of us could hear a sound. We didn't have to.

Taking a page from his playbook, I made both my hands into circular saws and worked them into both sides of his neck. Once his head was separated from his body, the advantage might turn to my side. But I was sloppy when I did that. Real sloppy.

While my hands were busy, Henry made an axe from one of his and cracked my head open. Right down the center line.

He had Crashed me.

He had Crashed me.

Not a very deep groove, true. But...

...I could feel my essence slipping out into whatever was the Deepness...

...and I had lost.

I had lost.

But somehow, in that very Void moment, with not a hope in hell within grabbing distance, I heard something. True, without sound, without a communicator, there was no way I could have heard anything. No way.

I heard Henry's laughter.

Laugh at me, would he? Laugh at me?

I sent substance up from my body towards my head. What substance I could reach, I grabbed and stuffed back inside my cranium. And I formed a protective dome over that crack and sent substance bands around my whole head to hold it together.

The unmatrixed scum couldn't believe what he was seeing. That was okay by me.

I formed one of my fists into the shape of an anvil and knocked Henry's head off.

Henry's face, swooshing back with the head it was on, looked hurt, astonished, and vengeful. He stretched out one of his hands and made a great catch. He plunked it back on his neck and little tendrils came out to anchor it to his body. The fight wasn't over.

I was ready to charge in for the final scene when I felt something being slapped into my hand. There was a presence beside me, maybe behind me, but I was looking at what they'd put in my palm and five attached fingers.

It was a cybersurgeon's motor-scalpel.

Just as pretty as if it'd come off a tray in Norton's clinic, and just as effective. There was no need to turn it on. It came alive in my hand.

Henry had already started a charge, which was a very stupid thing to do under the present circumstances. Otherwise, I would have had to find a way to chase him, and that would have taken a much, much longer time.

He was starting to morph his body into something with as many stickers as a porcupine, only all of them bigger and deadlier. I picked my spot, managed to propel myself upward, and came down with the motor-scalpel. It would have been nice to hear it buzz.

It would have been even nicer to hear the sound as it cut into the center of Henry's head and cleaved it into two equal pieces. One fell to the left, the other to the right.

Each half had fifty percent of a very surprised expression.

Henry's porcupined body hung limp below it. I began carving at the neck, so I could make sure he couldn't somehow pull himself together.

There was a grip on my upper arm and I finally was able to turn and see the gifter who had bequeathed me the magic motor-scalpel.

Alice.

Hanging right in the void, unharmed. Alice.

She pointed back at some figures in protective suits a distance away. One of them must have had the instrument on them, which wasn't a bad idea. That one had to have given it to her.

Alice tapped on the hand that held the motor-scalpel and pointed at herself. I handed her the thing. Once she gripped it, she got an expression so evil that even I was uncertain for a long moment.

She took hold of Henry's remains and began what would be an extensive period of eclectic surgery.

The first part she tackled was between his legs.

⋝-⋜

As might be expected, my band of brothers conducted both myself and Alice to safety. It turned out Henry had more than a few soldiers of his own, but he kept our vendetta private. The Ring had sent in their men, and it turned into one big Crash party. Our casualties were low, theirs were high.

Denny, Marlon, Percy, and Chuck were still functional, and mostly harm-free. I gave a silent prayer to Gates for that.

It seemed that the Deepness had lost a lot of tractive power due to Henry's meddling, otherwise I think Alice and me, and maybe Henry himself, would have been random data in its grip. The Deepness's power seemed to be increasing, though, and it took a helluva lot of tractor power to get us out of there. The boys, Alice, and I were the first to emerge, and I held her hand and gave the crowds behind the Cop barriers the V-for-victory sign. Alice raised her own fist and smiled. The onlookers shouted, stomped, whistled, and made other good noises. The Cops looked mighty pleased, too.

I was tired, and hurting. Alice and a uniformed Denny supported me as I walked away from the Deepness, where Ring agents were still emerging. Kelly was near the barriers, but he was walking towards us and we towards him.

"Joe," said Denny, "you got him."

"Correction, Denny," I said. "We got him." I hugged Alice harder with my one arm and she nuzzled the side of my face. Every step made me think someone had put neutronium in my shoes.

Kelly took very long steps over towards us, not morphing so as not to startle the crowd. He grabbed me by the sides of my head and, once again, smiled. "Joe, well done."

"Thanks. What about that Pulse he talked about? Said it was activated."

"That recording you put in Alice's hands was what we needed, Joe," he stared joyfully at me. "We were able to track it to the source and dampen it."

"By how much?"

A huge thrumming noise gradually became audible. All of us looked around, trying to see where it was coming from.

Then a huge BOOM of noise happened, and most of us were knocked off our feet.

Kelly caught my eye as we were getting up.

"About that much," he said.

>-<

This time, they assured me, Henry hadn't been able to transfer into another body or receptacle. They monitored every emanation coming from that pit, and blocked whatever seemed a transmission. Around the time I Crashed Henry, they recorded such an occurrence. It hit the shield, rebounded, and died.

Hopefully, so did Henry. We brought his remains up and the remains remain in some department belonging to the Ring. What Alice and I did to him seems to preclude any villainous resurrection.

But it seems you never know.

You just never really know.

Naturally, I had to report in to Norton, as did several of my comrades. He was speechless when he saw me. Norton put me under, did his tinkering, and brought me back. My head felt a lot better.

"Three weeks in hospital," he ordered. "Guards at every entry point. You stay there. Three weeks."

"Thanks, Nort, but I thought Alice and i—"

"Three. Weeks."

So I didn't argue with him.

Denny and Alice kept me company as I healed. They were on either side of the hoverbed I was in, with the sensors connected to my cranium drawing interesting patterns on the monitor screen. Especially when Alice was near.

Den had lost what amounted to a hand in the battle with Henry's soldiers, and Norton had to feed him enough substance for him to regenerate it properly. He seemed to have lost a little of his gosh-wow attitude since getting that off-scarlet badge of courage. But he still gave proper thanks to Gates for bringing us through the battle, and I don't blame him a bit.

He also said he'd called the Chinese Cabal and told them my enemy was dead. Somehow, I think the Octorad got the message.

Alice was, as might be expected, scarred by her ordeal. It would take a lot of cycles for her to damp down the memory of what Henry had done to her, if she even could. She held me, hugged me, even kissed me. But there was no talk of plugging. Not yet.

On the eve of the third week's ending, as Norton would have predicted, I was feeling great enough to have them unhook the monitor leads from my head. The pain blocks I left alone, but I could perambulate a bit myself, and I did. So I was standing up with one hand on the head of the hoverbed when I addressed Alice and Denny.

"I've had a little time to get the relay rust out of my head. So let me talk to both of you, one at a time. Okay?"

Denny said, "Sure, Joe. What?"

Alice kept silent, but gave consent with her eyes.

"Let's start with you, Denny. Do I have to tell you that you handled yourself exceptionally well in this caper?"

"Aw, Joe, I went into botch mode so many times..."

"Shut that stuff up, kid, or I'll botch you myself. You were green, sure, but you pulled off some moves from the start even I hadn't considered. When it counted, you performed. At the end, you took down enemy troops, they tell me."

"Well..."

"Point being, Den, I'm not getting younger. Not in the ROM and RAM, anyway. Want to make you an offer. Not a high-paying one yet. You know what my budget is like. But it'd be a chance to hone your talents, take on more cases, learn whatever more you can, and help me out. Capeesh?"

"Work for you?"

"That's the size of it."

He tried to rush me but I put my hand on his chest to stop him. "Is that answer in the affirmative, Den?"

"Affirmative and yes double-plus and I accept, Joe!"

I smiled and clapped him on the shoulder. "We'll tack you on an office soon. Alice, tomorrow I want you to draw up papers for Denny. But we have another matter, first."

She probably knew what I was going to say. But she waited for me to say it.

"Alice, will you marry me?"

I saw the start of a tear in her left eye. "Affirmative, Joe."

At that, Denny walked back, touched the wall plate in the room, and the doors opened. A moderately huge bunch of folks entered, including Kelly, my old Chief, Marlon, Percy, Chuck, and, wouldn't you know it, Father Jonas. They all yelled "Surprise!" or "Congratulations!" or something like that.

"Greetings, Joe," the priest opened a Book of Gates as he spoke. "Your partner let us know about this. We've been waiting for you. Why don't we do the job right here?"

When I found my voice, I turned to Alice. "Whaddyou think, babe?"

Smiling, she put her arms around my neck. "Shouldn't have to ask."

As the priest got to work, I wondered when Alice and I would consummate our marriage.

When the time came, I figured she'd know.

And I'd know, too.

THE END

ABOUT OUR CREATORS

WRITER

LOU MOUGIN - despite rumors to the contrary, is a writer. In prose, he's written the Frankenstein novel, MONSTER IN THE MANSIONS, and several other items for ProSe Press. His first Joe the Computer story debuted in Airship27's LEGENDS OF NEW PULP FICTION. SECONDARY SUPERHEROES OF GOLDEN AGE COMICS, a history of lesser-known 1940s comic heroes, has been published by McFarland Books. In comics, his current gig is scripting horror stories for Warrant's THE CREEPS, SHUDDER, and VAMPIRESS CARMILLA. He's also written stories for Marvel, Eclipse, AC Comics, InDellible, Claypool, Lucky, and others. (What others? At this point, he's not sure himself!) This is his first ever detective-type book. If you buy it, he'll be exceedingly happy. If not, he'll probably cry for a week.

ARTIST

FER CALVI - was born in Córdoba, Argentina, in 1973. He lives in Buenos Aires, where he has worked in illustration, animation and comics for thirty years. He has illustrated dozens of books and covers. His comics and illustrations have appeared in various newspapers and magazines. He has published numerous comic books and 13 graphic novels. His work has been published in Italy, France, Spain, Norway, UK and the USA. He lives with his wife, Maia, surrounded by books, magazines and rabbits.

www.ingramcontent.com/pod-product-compliance
Lightning Source LLC
Chambersburg PA
CBHW051129260626
47170CB00005B/1738